A Candlelight Ecstasy Romance™

"DON'T WHAT, CAT?"

His breath caressing her face, he bent toward her with the deliberate maddening slowness she remembered so well. His lips came close, then moved away—tantalizing hers until she ached for the warm possession of his mouth. His lips brushed hers as he murmured, "We've both been waiting for this and you know it." There was a husky catch of amusement in his voice. "Your body remembers mine, honey, and you want me as much as I want you. . . ."

BRAND OF PASSION

Shirley Hart

A CANDLELIGHT ECSTASY ROMANCE™

Published by
Dell Publishing Co., Inc.
1 Dag Hammarskjold Plaza
New York, New York 10017

ISBN: 0–440–10324–X

Printed in the United States of America
First printing—January 1983

To Our Readers:

We have been delighted with your enthusiastic response to Candlelight Ecstasy Romances™, and we thank you for the interest you have shown in this exciting series.

In the upcoming months we will continue to present the distinctive sensuous love stories you have come to expect only from Ecstasy. We look forward to bringing you many more books from your favorite authors and also the very finest work from new authors of contemporary romantic fiction.

As always, we are striving to present the unique, absorbing love stories that you enjoy most—books that are more than ordinary romance.

Your suggestions and comments are always welcome. Please write to us at the address below.

Sincerely,

The Editors
Candlelight Romances
1 Dag Hammarskjold Plaza
New York, New York 10017

CHAPTER ONE

The spring day had drizzled into a peculiar, half-bright, half-dark dusk. Fog hung like a miasma over the streets of Chicago, but here and there a car drove unknowingly through the gray mist without lighted headbeams. Catriona Morgan clenched the wheel of her gray VW and struggled to concentrate on her driving. With a mood as dark as the weather, she swung into the parking lot of the Paradise Club, her headlights illuminating the moisture-beaded surface of club owner Nick Armand's black limousine. She parked beside the large car and turned off the motor. Clouds hung over the red-tiled roof of the club, and at the corners of the peaked facade rain spilled over the eaves. It was the last day of April—and she still hadn't heard from Logan Blake . . .

But suppose there was an answer to her letter, hanging from the message board, waiting for her! She opened the car door and dashed for the sheltered entryway. She was gasping when she reached its dry shelter. Under the protective awning there was safety from the rain, but in the misty dusk the wind whipped her dark hair across her face and wrapped her black velvet skirt around her slender ankles. She shivered uncontrollably. If Logan hadn't answered her letter by today . . . she would have to call him.

At that disturbing thought her hands trembled and her stomach felt as if it were tied in knots. Distracted, she forgot that first step up at the doorway and caught the heel of her gold sandal on the threshold. "Damn," she swore softly, and stumbled forward into the red and black foyer.

Peggy, the hostess, chuckled huskily. In the soft light of the club Catriona could see the blond girl perched like a purple owl on her stool, her eyes flickering over Catriona, taking in the worn gray coat and the blown tangle of dark hair. Peggy was younger than Catriona's twenty-seven and loved her job. The girl was an unlikely combination of hard-bitten business woman and tall sex kitten. She could add up the figures on a check faster than an adding machine, and she loved to dress just at the edge of blatant sexuality. Tonight she had on a purple jump suit with harem trouser legs. The jump suit had a halter neckline that tied around her throat and covered everything in front quite discreetly, but Catriona had seen that particular garment before and knew that when the girl turned around, every square inch of her back was naked to the top of her derriere. Catriona had seen Nick's hand linger at that low bare spot while he stood ostensibly talking to the girl about some minor point that needed her attention in the dining room.

Peggy's opinion of Catriona's coat was written all over her face. *I'm a disappointment to her,* Catriona thought sardonically. *She thinks I should come in wearing a black velvet cape. That's what she would do if she were the singer.* Four years ago Catriona might have considered it. Now, clothes were unimportant.

She picked up the hem of her black skirt to walk across the red-carpeted floor toward Peggy. Her voice carefully casual, she asked, "Any messages for me?" Peggy turned to the corkboard behind her and flipped over the three sheets pinned there. Her fingernails were painted a dark red. A pale expanse of bare back was visible. She turned back again and shook her head. "No, nothing. What were you expecting, a message from your lover?"

Catriona's nails curled into her palms, but she kept her face carefully blank. "That's not likely, is it?" She pivoted away and walked across the dance floor toward the back of the stage, aware that Peggy's curious eyes were burning into her back.

Inside the tiny dressing room she took off her coat and hung it on the long bar. Her dressing table was lit all around with bulbs like that of a movie star. Nick had insisted on that, and she supposed she should be grateful. She stared into the mirror for a second, then sat down and began to apply the makeup that would take away that washed-out look. Too many late nights, too much worry, too much trouble—and not enough money. She picked up the green eye shadow and ran it lightly around her eyes, then covered it with a shimmering gold that would shine in the spotlight. Eyeliner and mascara darkened the already thick lashes. Blusher took away the ghostly look. She ran a comb through her dark shoulder-length hair, and stood up to tug at the black knit triangle across her small, high breasts. It was cut to cover one shoulder and to leave the other arm and shoulder completely bare and was long enough to reach her waist and merge with the black skirt, making it look like a gown. Her father had taught her how to dress and make the most of her average height, pale skin, and dark hair. The thought brought a sting of pain. He had been loving, artistic—and impractical. Money had never been important to him. "We have enough, darlin'," he'd say in that Irish brogue he could use when the mood struck him. "Enough for us and a bit left over for a drop now and again." No, money had not been a life-or-death matter then.

She went out of the room and walked down the hall to

the main dining room. Ken, the piano player in the band, was up on the small stage, fiddling with the sound board, trying to set the levels at a lower volume. They'd had complaints last night.

He spared her a quick look. "Go stand toward the back, Cat, and see if you think this is too loud."

Accustomed to his peremptory tone, she crossed the floor and stood in the back among the empty tables. Ken was something of a worrier. He was this way before every performance, his face a thundercloud of anticipated doom, even though they had a perfectly competent soundman. Now he played full chords on the Fender electric piano and glanced across the room at her nervously.

The music died away. "Sounds all right to me. Aren't the monitors working?" she asked.

Ken ran a hand through his sandy hair. "I think so. I'm not sure, though. God, I remember the day when you didn't need a degree in electrical engineering to be a musician."

As she came back across the floor, he gave up his nervous adjusting of the volume levels on the electric piano and settled down at the baby grand, a distinct look of relief on his face, his hands finding the soft, unusual chord progression of "When Sunny Gets Blue." Ken had talent, far more than he utilized. His eyes flickered over her as she walked toward him and leaned into the curve of the piano. "Anything new on Robbie?" he asked, his fingers continuing to drift over the keys, his eyes moving over her.

She shook her head. He gave her a long, searching look. "You'd better get a grip on yourself. You look like hell."

"Thanks," she said shortly. "You're so good for my ego."

"I could be," he said softly. The chords on the piano melted into a soft rhumba beat. "I've got you under my skin," the piano sang, and Catriona smiled.

She shook her head, her smile still on her lips. "We've been over that ground before."

The music shifted again, and he began to play "Endless Love." She laughed softly. "You're hopeless."

He stopped playing. "I haven't got much money, you know that, Cat, but you're welcome to what I have—"

"No," she said quickly. "It's out of the question."

His fingers went instinctively back to the piano. "Heard anything from Blake?"

"No," she said huskily. "I guess I should have known better."

Ken's shoulders moved under the velvet evening jacket and one sandy eyebrow lifted. "A rich rancher from Wyoming? He was worth a try." His mouth twisted. "After all, the end justifies the means."

There was a harsh quality in his voice that disturbed her. Shortly after her affair with Logan, Ken's sympathetic comment one night on her haggard appearance had led to her eventual confiding in him. After that Ken had been a friend—a good friend—but nothing more. She had been burned once; she did not want to be burned again. Ken wanted more than friendship, she knew that. But he hadn't pressed her and it had developed into a running joke between them.

The rest of the band arrived; Morrey, clutching his guitar case protectively; Bill, incredibly organized and neat, carrying his drumsticks and mallets in immaculate black cases.

Morrey walked too close to the high hat cymbals and his case caught the edge of them. The clatter and clash brought Bill's irritable: "Watch it, you klutz. You knock over that set of Zildjians and you'll buy the replacements."

Tempers and nerves were always on edge before they performed. Tom worked on the soundboard, while Catriona placed the microphone on the stand and adjusted it to the proper angle. Ken preferred to use instrumentals only for the first set, while people were coming in, ordering, getting settled with a drink. He had respect for Catriona's talent, perhaps more than she did herself. She had been grateful for Ken's willingness to hire her. Two years ago her singing had been erratic, good one night, not good the next. Every song was fraught with painful memories. But in the end she had conquered her emotions and had returned to the stage. Singing was all she knew how to do.

She stepped out and walked over to the piano. Ken stood up and kissed her. His lips were cool on hers and aroused no emotion in her at all. The good-luck kiss that had begun as a joke had metamorphosed into a ritual. Ken occasionally took advantage of the public nature of their embrace to deepen the kiss. He did that tonight, and Catriona unobtrusively put her palms on his chest and gave him a little push.

By the end of the evening faint wisps of smoke curled in the air, and soft laughter came from behind the glare of the spotlight. The band was into the last set, and it was her turn to sing. She fought an overwhelming sense of desolation. *Concentrate on the lyrics,* she told herself fiercely.

Her voice felt and sounded husky, but the huskiness only added to the sensuality of the song. The black velvet of her skirt rustled as she swayed in front of the mike. Alone in the circle of light, she tried desperately to recreate the lyrics of the song—the story of a woman caught in the throes of a love affair.

When two o'clock came and the band began to pack up, she was only too glad to leave the stand and go back to the room to get her coat. She decided to go out the back door to avoid the inquisitive looks from Peggy. She thrust her arms into her coat, went out of the room and down the hall in the other direction, toward the heavy fire door that opened out onto a half flight of stairs that led to the parking lot.

Ken followed her out. He walked behind her down the stairs, and next to the vapor lamp he caught her elbow. "Cat, seeing you like this . . . if there's anything at all I can do . . ."

She lifted her head toward him. His features in the light were dear and familiar. "There's nothing you can do."

He grasped her shoulders and turned her toward him. "Let me marry you, Cat. Let me take care of you. We'd find a way to borrow the money."

Catriona shook her head and smiled up into his face. "You're a crazy musician—you know that?"

He hesitated and then tightened his grasp. "I want you to know that I . . ." He bent his head and planted a hard kiss on her lips.

They had been alone in the parking lot among the dark shadows of the cars, but the sound of steps made Ken lift his head. The steps came closer.

And that was when she saw him.

From under the awning he moved easily toward her. Had she conjured him up out of her imagination because she wanted to see him so badly? No, his black hair moved from the same breeze that touched hers, and the broad thrust of shoulders under the navy topcoat could only belong to Logan Blake.

"It's him, isn't it?" Ken said softly.

"Yes. Please—you must go. Let me talk to him alone."

He stared at her for what seemed like an eternity. Then he said stubbornly, "I want to stay."

"No."

The fierce desperation in that one word made him drop his hands. Then he reached out and pressed his fingertips against her cheek. "I'm crazy to let you see him again. If it weren't for Robbie . . ."

"I'll call you as soon as I can," she promised quickly. "Now please go."

"I know how much this means to you, otherwise—"

"Go," she whispered harshly.

He stepped into his car. Almost at once the engine turned over and he was pulling out of the lot. And she was left to face Logan Blake alone.

In slow motion Logan took the last remaining steps that carried him to her. She stood very still, her hands trembling in the pockets of her coat.

"Sent your lover away, Catriona? You're very good at that, aren't you?" That male voice was just as husky and provocative as it had been two years ago.

Her knees shook, but she leaned against her car and smiled at him with an air of careless unconcern. "You never change, do you, Logan?" she said lightly. "No amenities, no how are yous, just straight to the point."

Just as he had been straight to the point the night he had delivered the ultimatum: *"If you love me . . . you won't let me go back to Wyoming alone."* Those words had torn her in two. She stood facing him with the words she had spoken to him two years ago echoing in her mind.

"Logan," she had whispered, *"please, just give me six months. That's all I need . . ."*

"But I need you—now."

The words had thrilled her, even though they had been cold, implacable. *"Please try to understand, Logan. You and I will have the rest of our lives together . . ."*

But they hadn't. And now they were facing each other impersonally across a dark parking lot like two people who didn't know each other at all.

He said, "I didn't come halfway across the country to argue with you."

"You didn't have to come to Chicago at all," she said bluntly.

"No, I didn't, did I?" he replied, his tone challenging. "Your letter made that quite clear." In the dim light of the overhead vapor lamp, his hair shone devil-dark. "But I do know the way to Chicago."

The night air crackled between them like the turbulent air of a coming thunderstorm. "I must admit," he drawled, "I was—curious. You must be in serious trouble to ask me for help."

"I'm not in trouble . . ."

A breeze whipped a small shred of paper which caught in her hair. He reached forward. Before she had time to shrink from his touch, he plucked the paper out of her dark hair and tossed it away. Then he said, "Can't we go somewhere warm and comfortable to discuss this?"

She didn't want to go anywhere warm and comfortable with him. But . . . "We can go to my apartment if you like—"

"My motel room is closer." There was an intentness in his voice that she remembered well.

For two long, lonely years she had tried to delude herself into thinking he meant nothing to her. But this was worse, much worse, than she had expected. She had hoped to avoid seeing him entirely, but if he meant to badger her, she had no choice. She had to take whatever punishment he cared to mete out. She had to think of Robbie.

"Well," he mocked her. "Are you going to give me a ride?"

She fought to stay coolly polite. "Yes, of course."

She climbed into the driver's seat, and he got in the other side. The little foreign car suddenly became very small. He eased his long legs under the dash and made himself comfortable in a way so reminiscent of that first time that her throat closed. He laid his head back against the headrest. Uncannily, he murmured softly, "This appeals to my sense of the ironic, Catriona," then tersely told her the name of the motel.

She gritted her teeth and started the car. As long as she was at the wheel, she told herself, everything was all right. She was in control. But her heart pounded erratically when she reached for the gear shift because her fingers brushed the soft corduroy of his trousers, and the well-remembered scent of his after-shave drifted to her nose. Luckily, the traffic wasn't heavy at that hour, and in minutes Catriona reached the motel parking lot and turned the small car into the driveway.

"Number thirty-four," he murmured without lifting his head. She gripped the wheel and slowed the car to trail it along the low brick building, peering under the little coach lanterns to find the right number.

A dark blue sedan sat in front of Logan's door. It was evidently a rental car. He must have taken a taxi to the club. "Pull in the space across from my room," he ordered her, and she had no choice but to obey.

When she had the car in neutral, he reached for the switch and turned off the motor. The keys disappeared into his pocket. She stared into his shadowed face. His smile mocked her. "Too many repetitions of our first meeting might become boring."

He got out of the car and came around to her side. His hand on her elbow, he escorted her across the tarmac. Another key appeared in his hand, and then she was pushed gently into the room. "You don't seem as eager as you were that night."

He snapped on the light. She took a step into the middle of the room, hugged her arms around her waist, and felt chilled and frightened. There was an undercurrent of menace in his voice she had never heard before—and it suddenly occurred to her that though they had been lovers two years ago, she didn't know Logan Blake very well at all. He threw the key on the desk with a snap of his wrist and she jumped.

His eyes narrowed on her. "Bit nervous, aren't you?" He shrugged out of his coat and tossed it on the bed. The cutting blue glance of his eyes swept over her and his mouth twisted. "Cold?"

He knew why she clutched the coat tightly around her.

"Yes . . . no . . ." Disturbed by her own conflicting emotions, she turned away and stood staring at the window, which was tightly covered by a drawn drape. "Logan, please don't." The plea came out in a low, husky tone.

"Having trouble with your throat?"

She didn't bother to deny it. Singing had been difficult all evening. Worrying about Robbie had tightened her throat. "Yes."

She continued to stand with her back to him. There was a silence, then a clink of glass against glass. "I thought your last song sounded as if you were pushing it. Here, take this." He came to stand behind her. "You sound as if you need it."

She hadn't known he was in the club. The thought of him watching her without her knowing it made her reach for the glass. The liquor was a potent brandy and it warmed her throat all the way down. She handed the glass back to him. "Thank you."

His eyes flickered over her briefly before he turned and set the glass on the desk. Then he pivoted around toward her, leaned against the furniture, folded his arms—and waited.

She had to begin, but she couldn't think how. "I—do you mind if I sit down?"

He didn't move a muscle. "Be my guest."

There was a table by the window and two black vinyl chairs. She sat in one of them, put her hands on the table, and laced them together to keep them from trembling. She didn't look at him. "I need ten thousand dollars."

The silence in the room seemed to ring in her ears.

He spoke one soft word. "Why?"

"I need it—for a friend."

There was another long pause. "A male friend?"

She clutched at the straw. If Logan believed she had another lover, she could salvage her pride. "Yes," she said huskily.

The click of glass sounded again, and when she turned her head to look at him, she saw that he had poured another drink—for himself this time. He raised the glass to his mouth, took a long swallow, then lowered it and stood staring down into it for a moment. When she thought his silence would drive her mad, he lifted cool eyes to her. "What made you think I would loan you that kind of money?"

She spread her hands in an expressive gesture. "You're the only one I know who has that kind of money."

"I'm rather unique in your company of friends then, aren't I?"

His dark gaze unnerved her. "Will you—are you going to consider it?" She raised glittering eyes to him.

His gaze was slicing. "What do you have for collateral?"

"I . . ." The thought crossed her mind that she could pretend ignorance of the meaning of the word, but one glance at his face warned her not to. "I have my paycheck. I could sign over a percentage of my wage . . ."

"You're a three-hundred-dollar-a-week singer, Cat. How long do you think it would take you to pay back ten thousand dollars?"

"The rest of my life, probably," she murmured.

He said coolly, "But you'd do that for this—male friend?"

"Yes," she said, without hesitation.

His fingers tightened around the glass. A car pulled up outside the motel, and she heard the laughing voices of the men and women as they got out of the car. The outside noise only intensified the quiet in the room where she sat. Logan's dark face could have been set in stone.

She clenched her teeth in helpless frustration. She had known the whole thing was hopeless from the beginning. But she had been desperate—so desperate she had written to the man she had thought she would never want to see

again. She got up out of the chair, her shoulders drooping. "I'll go now. Give me my keys, Logan."

He turned away from her and set the glass down on the table with a click. "Is the money for Fowler?"

Her whole body froze with shock. "Ken? No—no!"

He straightened away from the desk. "Then the answer is yes."

Her eyes blazed with joyous relief. "Oh, Logan, I—"

"On one condition."

The elation in her eyes faded and changed to wary watchfulness. "A condition?"

His eyes began a slow path over her, and even though she still wore her coat, she felt as if he were touching her physically—as he once had . . . "You said you were willing to sign over a portion of your paycheck for the rest of your life." He took a step toward her and involuntarily she stiffened. But she stood her ground and gazed back at him. Even with her heart pounding in fear and anticipation, she could see that he had lost none of his physical charisma or male charm. If anything, two years had intensified his virility. He was good-looking in the best sense of the word, his features shaped by character and maturity. His nose was fine boned and well-shaped, his chin firm and square. He wore a suede vest over his Western shirt, and his pants were a brown corduroy, cut to fit his lean hips.

"Yes, I said that. And I meant it. Do you want a lawyer to—"

"No." He reached out to touch her, his fingertip tracing the rise of her cheekbone. She wanted to gasp with shock, but she couldn't. She could only fight down her emotional response and pretend his touch didn't affect her in the slightest. "I don't want your money." His hand dropped to the soft, vulnerable base of her throat. "I want you."

Stinging pain whipped around her body as if she had been dropped naked straight down into the icy waters of

Lake Michigan. "You swine! I wouldn't sleep with you for a million dollars!"

"Does that mean your answer is no?"

"Yes," she hissed at him. "Yes."

She turned to run from the room, but his hard hands caught her shoulders and he pulled her back against him. "You've slept with me before. Why are you drawing the line now?" He turned her in his arms and watched her futile struggles with a gleaming satisfaction in his blue eyes.

Exhausted and on the verge of tears, she saw his head lowering, his lips seeking her temple. "Logan, please—please don't."

He shifted his grip slightly. His hand low on her back, he pressed her body against his until she could feel every muscular inch of him. He lifted her face to his and examined her tear-bright eyes without a flicker of compassion in his own. "Don't what, Cat?" His breath caressing her face, he bent toward her with a deliberate and maddening slowness she remembered well. His lips came close and then moved away, tantalizing hers until she ached for the warm possession of his mouth. His lips brushed hers as he murmured, "We've both been waiting for this, and you know it." There was a husky catch of amusement in his voice. "Your body remembers mine, honey, and you want me as much as I want you—"

Desperately, she strained her arms, trying to put distance between them. "No!" She wanted to push him away, her mind ordered her to, but his mouth closed over hers and she melted into him like spun candy. His probing tongue crossed the barrier of her teeth and found the sweetness of every corner of her mouth. His hands moved over the thin wool of her coat, and a low sound of impatience escaped him.

He lifted his head and stared at her, his hands hard on

her upper arms. "You want me as much as I want you," he repeated, and then added harshly, "admit it, Catriona."

"I loathe you." Her voice was scathing.

He let her go and she walked to the door. She had her hand on the knob when she remembered her keys. She turned around again to find his eyes running over her in a disturbing fashion. "Forget something?" he asked.

"My keys," she said huskily.

His hand went inside his pocket, but he didn't bring the keys out. "What do you need the money for, Cat?"

She said hotly, "That's none of your business."

He gave her a long, considering look. "There is another alternative."

"Alternative?" She watched him warily.

"Suppose I offer you a job—a legitimate job."

She stared at him in disbelief. "What kind of a job?"

"I always hire part-time help for the summer season."

The hope that had risen in her fell again. "You mean you want me to rustle cows?"

The side of his mouth quirked. "Herd, not rustle."

"That's as ridiculous as your first offer."

"Is it?" He studied her under dark lashes. "You seem to think I should just hand you the money and walk away."

"No—I thought you would agree to take a portion of my salary."

"You thought wrong."

"Well, so did you. I couldn't possibly be a—a cowboy. I don't know anything about cows and I've never ridden a horse."

"In that case"—he thrust his hand into his pocket and brought it out with the keys dangling from his fingers—"I guess I can't help you."

His cool blandness made her want to fly at him. A sudden vision of Robbie's tousled red hair floated in front of her eyes. "How long?" she asked.

"How long—what?" His words were soft, but if they carried an innuendo, she ignored it.

"How long would I have to work for you?" she asked insistently.

"Through the season."

"Which ends in—August?"

"November," he said, his eyes hooded.

"November! You can't be serious—"

"If you sign on with me, you start now and you work until the first of November."

There was a long moment of silence. Mentally, she counted the months in her mind. Eight of them, she thought in dismay. But measured against all the years of Robbie's life, it was a short time, indeed.

She forced her eyes back to Logan's face. It was hard and implacable. There was not a flicker in those cool blue eyes that betrayed the fact that he had asked her to be his mistress only moments ago. How could he switch his emotions off and on like that? To him, she supposed, a body was used for pleasure or work—whichever was the most beneficial at the moment. A chill of fear prickled along her spine. But she had no choice, not really. "All right," she said, and lifted her chin to face him, every bit of her Irish spirit and courage flying. "Yes. I'll take the job."

If he felt any satisfaction, it didn't show. He didn't move a muscle.

She asked, "How soon can you give me the money?"

"I can get the money wired here by Monday afternoon. Is that soon enough?" The question was bland.

"Yes—yes, that's soon enough." She paused, knowing she was utterly insane. "I'd like to go home, now. I'll take my keys."

He held out them out, the key chain looped over his lean fingers. Fighting the instinctive reaction of her body to his nearness, she reached out and slipped the chain off. She felt incredibly relieved when he folded his arms again and kept his lazy position against the desk. But when she turned to go, his soft voice stopped her. "Cat."

Her hand on the doorknob, she turned. "Yes?"

"There is one stipulation." He straightened up and came toward her. She couldn't move. She was caught in his aura of power and maleness.

"What is it?" she asked, her voice husky.

"If you can't take the work on the range"—there was a silence and then he finished softly—"we'll go back to my original offer."

She stiffened. "Isn't that called sexual harassment on the job?"

"There's no harassment. You either agree and take the money—or don't agree and leave it."

Her temper flared. "I'll take it, but I'll herd your damn cows till hell freezes over before I—" Her anger choked her and she turned and jerked at the door. It flew open and she stepped out into the night air and took a deep sobbing breath of relief—when she realized Logan was right behind her.

At the sound of the closing door she whirled. "What do you think you're doing?" she asked.

"Following you home."

"Oh, no, you're not," she said stiffly. "I'm perfectly capable of—"

"I know what you're perfectly capable of," he mocked. "Go on and get that car started—unless you want to spend the rest of the night here with me."

Her temper blazing, she stalked to the car. She was determined to lose him. She pulled out of the driveway and gunned the motor, and remembered with satisfaction that in the two years since their affair she had moved to another apartment. She had a good chance of losing him. But though she made several quick turns without signaling, the blue car followed her relentlessly.

She knew that even the dark could not hide the shabby condition of the house. She pulled up next to the curb and parked. The glare of lights in her rearview mirror told her Logan had done the same.

When she stepped up onto the sidewalk, he was beside her. "What are you doing?"

His answer was a firm grip on her elbow. "You're living here?" There was a husky growl of disbelief in his voice.

"Yes," she said. She stood for a moment, waiting for him to let go of her. When he didn't, she moved impatiently. "Let go of my arm."

"I'll go inside with you."

"I can take care of myself," she flared.

He didn't argue. He merely started walking forward. The hard, unyielding grip on her elbow forced her to stumble along beside him. "Will you let go of me?" she muttered heatedly.

He didn't answer or slacken his pace. The wind had died away and the air felt warmer. As they walked up the half flight of stairs and crossed the wooden porch, their steps mingled with the sound of a jet plane whining overhead. At the door Logan released her arm and she unlocked the entryway door. Before she could close it, he followed her inside.

With an acrid bitterness she knew now that Logan meant to stay for the night. She turned to him, her barely controlled anger making her voice shake. "You've seen me home. Now please go."

"Where's your apartment? Top floor?" With gentle firmness he took hold of her and guided her toward the stairs. Her throat filled with helpless fury. She led the way up, her nerves screaming awareness of him with every step she took.

On the third-flight landing in front of her door she turned to him. "I won't sleep with you, Logan," she said flatly. "If you're going to use force, I can't stop you, but—"

"Open the door."

Her heart pounding with fear and fury, she slipped the key into the lock. With a twist of the wrist she had it open. She stepped inside and flipped on the light, frantically trying to think of a way to lock him out, when he followed her through and closed the door. Then in one lightning move he had her pressed back against it, his lean body trapping her. Even through her coat she could feel the muscled strength of his thighs, the hardness of his chest pressed against her breasts. She had goaded him to anger, and the realization sent a fiery excitement racing around her body. He stared down at her, his eyes a deep cobalt blue. "Why would I use force," he asked, his voice silky, "when you've always been more than willing to give me what I want . . ."

Like a small animal who only realizes the danger after the trap is closed, she stared up into the tanned face and watched it come slowly closer. "No—"

He swooped and captured her half-open mouth and gained entrance instantly. Moist and warm and enticing, his tongue explored hers—and brought pleasure everywhere it touched. The weight of his hard body against her was a remembered pleasure. The wild, fierce delight she had always felt in Logan's arms bubbled through her veins. She lifted her arms to let her hands fight under his coat and vest to the shirt beneath. Hardly conscious of the urgency of her hands, she separated his shirt from his pants and pressed her palms against the bare skin of his back.

He lifted his lips enough to murmur with a soft chuckle, "Your hands are cold, honey."

She moved to draw her hands away, but he stopped her with the clamping pressure of his arms. "No," he murmured, "leave them there." He eased away from her slightly to allow him access to the buttons of her coat. She made a small protesting moan and twisted to get away, but his lower body and powerful thighs pressed her back against the door. Under his hands her coat fell open and the creamy expanse of skin above the knit top was exposed. Swiftly, he drew her coat down over her shoulders and relaxed his pressure against her lower body enough to allow the coat to fall to the floor. Almost at the same time he bent to press a kiss above her breast, on skin left bare by the slanting cut of her top. A sudden erotic chill shook her. Her body seemed to remember the warm contour of his lips.

She didn't want to remember. She dared not. Logan's kiss and touch would annihilate her. She moved, trying to force her unwilling hands to push him away, when his mouth settled over hers. Rising desire made her throat vibrate with a soft sound of need. When he heard that sound, he raised his head and a slow smile lifted his lips. Gently, he eased himself away from her until she was completely free.

"Now," he said gently, "tell me I'd have to use force to take you."

Hot anger flooded her. He had kissed and caressed her cold-bloodedly to prove his point. "Get out."

"Is that any way to talk to your future employer?"

She glared at him, her eyes shimmering with anger. "I want you out of here."

"Sorry," he said, in a voice that belied the word. "I'm spending the night."

"You can go to hell."

A glint of amusement flashed in his eyes. "And you'd help me along the way, wouldn't you?"

"Wouldn't I?" The anger in her eyes was mixed with a wicked amusement.

"I'll need my rest before the trip," he mocked.

"You're not staying here," she said flatly, no longer amused.

"I've slept on the range—I think I can manage the couch," he countered smoothly, as if she were a hostess offering him less-than-comfortable accommodations. "All I need is an extra blanket."

"Don't pretend you're concerned about me," she told him scathingly.

"All right, I won't. Now, are you going to get me a blanket—or shall I take one off your bed?"

A heavy weariness seemed to wash over her. Weeks of worrying about Robbie had fragmented her sleep. The confrontation with Logan had drained her. She felt nothing more than a strong desire to get into bed and lay her head on the pillow and let him do whatever he wanted to do. "There's a blanket in the closet," she said. "I'll get it." She went inside the tiny bedroom and found the blanket. She handed it to him. "The bathroom is just off the kitchen." He smiled and she turned her back to him, closing the door of the bedroom behind her.

She let him use the bathroom first, and after she heard him return, she put on her robe and walked through the living room, ignoring him. After she had cleaned her teeth and washed her face, she circled around through the living room again. He was already tucked under the blanket, but she could see his dark stockinged feet extended over the edge of the couch arm. *Damn it,* she thought, *he doesn't have to sleep here. He could have gone back to his motel room!* But when she went in and lay down, it seemed comforting to know that—for the first time in two years—she was not alone during the late-night hours.

CHAPTER TWO

She awoke to the sound of a male voice talking. Logan's voice. He was on the telephone. She couldn't hear the words, but she could hear the rise and fall of his deep voice as he talked, and she lay there wrapped in the warmth of the bed covers and the soothing murmur of his words and was amazed at how good she felt. She had, surprisingly enough, slept well. She felt lazily rested, like a cat that has had a long nap in the sun. Logan's voice stopped and the receiver made a thump into the wall. He had finished his call. Her eyelids drooped and she dozed . . .

The phone pealed sharply. She came awake with a start to hear it stop abruptly in the middle of the second ring. Logan's voice again, but there was a different quality about it this time. The deep voice had taken on the smooth cutting edge of Toledo steel, rapier-sharp and cool. Whom was he talking to?

The digital clock rolled over. 11:45. It was nearly noon. Logan would have the money in a few hours. She threw back the covers. The lovely scent of hot coffee drifted to her nose. Her white terry robe pulled high around her throat and belted tightly at her waist, she went out into the living room. Logan was not there. He was in the kitchen, sitting at the small table, drinking coffee, looking far more rested and alert than he should have after spending a night on her too-short couch. His hair was shower damp, but his jaw was still dark with night beard.

She went through to the bathroom, and when she came out, he got to his feet and went unerringly to the cupboard to get her a cup. "Coffee?" he asked. "I remembered you like a cup first thing in the morning."

She ignored his reference to those intimate nights and lazy mornings they had spent together two years ago and took the hot cup from his hands. "Thank you."

He watched her for a moment. "We can't pick up the bank draft until four o'clock this afternoon," he told her. "We'll need to go and get some things for you before that. You'll have an hour or so to deliver the money to—wherever you want it to go." He glanced around the apartment and then back at her. "I assume this place came furnished."

She nodded. "I'll have to give notice."

"I've already arranged to leave your key and a month's rent with the woman downstairs." He rubbed a hand over his jaw and the soft rasp of hair against skin reached her ears. "I need to go back to the motel to pick up my suitcase and shave and change. Is there anything else we should do?"

Something about his coupling of them together disturbed her. "I have to pack and I'll have to tell Ken—"

The line of his jaw hardened. "Fowler called here this morning. I told him you were leaving."

"What did he say?"

"He insisted that you sing one set tonight. I agreed to that," he said casually. "How soon can you be ready to go?"

His arrogant arranging of her life annoyed her. "Go where?"

"Out to get some of the gear you'll need."

She rubbed her hands over the soft terry tie of her robe, taking comfort from its nubby texture. "I can't afford to buy anything."

His mouth lifted in a mocking smile. "I figured that."

"Logan, I can't ask you to spend any more money . . ."

"You'll need range gear, a sleeping bag, boots, jeans, and shirts. I don't think that will break me."

"I can't let you buy things for me . . ."

"I don't see that you have much choice, Cat."

When had she ever had a choice in anything that involved Logan? She got dressed, packed her clothes, and followed him out to his car. At the motel she waited in the rented blue sedan while he shaved and changed. When he came out carrying his bag, she reluctantly gave him directions to a shopping center. The large department store was already filled with bustling shoppers when they walked in. He guided her to the sportswear department and picked up jeans, shirts, and a warm jacket, deferring to her personal preference for three inexpensive knit T-shirts.

Logan drove without direction this time, turning into a small street of shops. They got out of the car and he took her elbow and guided her to a bootery. The smell of leather was heavy in the air when they walked inside, and the shop was cluttered with shelves filled with Western boots. Logan plucked a pair of thick socks from a revolving rack and told Catriona to sit down. Under the watchful eyes of an older, balding man, Logan rolled back the cuff of her cream-colored pants and held her ankle in one hand while he tugged the sock over her nylon-clad foot. She was still struggling with her own response to his warm hand on her when he went back to the shelves and studied the boots thoughtfully. Then he pointed to a pair of outrageously expensive ones in a dark oxblood color. "Those, I think," he told the man, who went to get them in Catriona's size.

"They're too expensive. Logan, I don't want them . . ."

He replied coolly, "You can't ride without boots."

And it was then, when the smooth boots were fitted on her feet, that she began to realize just exactly what she had agreed to do.

"We'll take those," Logan said, and the balding man nodded. The boots were laid back in the box on top of each other. Logan paid the astronomical sum without the flicker of an eyelash and tucked the large box under his arm. His hand on her elbow, he walked with her out of the shop.

Inside the car he said, "Fowler has agreed to sell your car for you. Don't forget to give him the registration tonight at the club. Do you have it with you?" She nodded. "Good," he said. "I've got to go to the bank and provide them with indentification. I'm not sure how long everything will take." There was a long silence and then he drawled, "Will you come inside with me or would you prefer to wait in the car?"

She caught her breath. "I'll wait." He got out of the car, a mocking smile lingering on his lips.

She tried not to watch his lean body move away and looked out on the street. A woman walked down the sidewalk, trying to hold her skirt down against the wind, her head turning to watch Logan. He was a man who would attract a woman's attention even on a busy city street, she thought ruefully. She turned her head. Yesterday's fog and rain had blown away. The sun was shining down through the high-rise office buildings. That had to be a good omen—didn't it?

Her heart beat heavily in her chest. She tried to forget why she was sitting in downtown Chicago in the late afternoon, with her suitcase in the back seat, and tried to block out of her mind the fact that Logan was withdrawing a very large sum from his bank account to place in her hands. The wheels were in motion now, and she couldn't stop them. Fifteen minutes passed, then twenty, then thirty. Her palms were wet with perspiration. Suppose he had run into trouble? Suppose there was a problem and Logan was unable to get the money?

He strode around the corner of the pale brick building, his dark hair lifting in the wind. She waited on tenterhooks, afraid that he was going to tell her he had not gotten the bank draft. But when he was in the car seated beside her, he murmured, "Where to from here?"

She gave him the address of Sheryl's apartment on the east side. He didn't ask the obvious question, and she volunteered no more about their destination. Outside the apartment house she said, "I won't be long."

"I'm going in with you."

"No."

A parking place appeared in front of the car and Logan pulled smoothly into it. Before she could move, he turned and grasped her wrist. "I'm going in with you," he repeated.

She glared at him in helpless frustration. "No," she said. "You can't."

"Why?" His eyes glittered. "Don't you want me to meet your latest lover?"

Inwardly, she flinched. "No—no, I don't. Now if you'll just give me the money . . ."

Lean fingers slid to the inside of his jacket pocket. He tossed a white envelope into her lap. She forgot Logan, forgot her own dilemma. Something seemed to break and shatter inside her. That envelope would make Robbie strong and whole . . .

A rush of gratitude filled her. "Logan—I—thank you."

He leaned back in the seat. "Your thanks might be a little premature."

She stared at him wordlessly, her heart pounding.

"What you're holding is a worthless piece of paper—until I endorse it," he said smoothly.

"You swine," she breathed. "It's none of your business—"

"But I'm curious," he said softly, "and it will cost you a great deal if you don't satisfy my curiosity—the entire amount of the check, in fact."

Fury choked her. He had planned it all carefully. He had had no intention of handing the money to her without knowing its destination. Resigned, she said wearily, "All right, on one condition, you must promise to say nothing to contradict me."

"You mean you don't want your male friend to know you're turning your life upside down for him," he said flatly.

She stiffened and then said, "Yes." She forced herself to meet the sardonic disdain in those glittering eyes, but there was nothing she could say to disabuse him.

"Don't worry," he said blandly. "I won't give your little game away." He studied her for a moment. She met the gaze of his blue eyes with her face composed. He could think what he liked.

After he had scrawled his signature on the back of the draft, she tucked it in her purse and climbed out of the car, her nerves quivering with tension. Conscious of him behind her, she pulled open the heavy oak door and stepped into the entryway. The balky intercom was working, and she called Sheryl. After the door buzzed, she entered the room that was once a large reception hall, sharply aware of the unfamiliar sound of Logan's booted feet on the marble floor following her.

The ancient elevator creaked noisily upward. Logan leaned against the back of it, his face impassive, his arms folded. When the elevator ground to a halt, Logan held the door back for her.

Sheryl answered her knock almost at once. She was a

vivacious redhead, but strain and worry had etched dark circles under her eyes and her skin had a translucent look. Her greeting was unchanged, as warm and effusive as ever. "Where have you been? I just tried to call you a little while ago."

Catriona stepped into the room with Logan behind her. "Sheryl, this is Logan Blake, my employer. Logan, my sister-in-law, Sheryl Morgan."

"Your employer?" Sheryl echoed. "But—"

Catriona glanced around the room and said quickly, "Where's the monster?"

"Asleep, thank God." Sheryl ran a long, thin hand through the profusion of red hair that swung out around her shoulders. "Come in, please, and sit down. You'll have to excuse the mess." This was directed to Logan. "I sell plants on weekends out of my home at parties and I just finished one."

Catriona sank down in the couch and let the sunny cheerfulness of her sister-in-law's apartment melt into her, even though she was conscious of Logan settling on the cushion next to her. The high-ceilinged spaciousness and sunlit, homey rooms outweighed the other inconveniences of the older apartment. Sheryl had decorated with white wicker furniture and dozens of plants, giving the place the atmosphere of a sunporch. A plant fiend, she grew them by the dozens and sold them in a little shop she shared with another girl who was a macrame expert. At the bay window spider plants in macrame hangers dripped green runners halfway to the floor, and African violets were in bloom, as well as yellow jonquils and red tulips on long stems that Sheryl had nurtured through the winter to bring to early bloom.

"I thought you were coming to the party," she said to Catriona, settling herself in the chair opposite them, her green gaze flickering over Logan's lean form.

Catriona laid her head back and closed her eyes. "I'm

sorry. I was tied up with other things." She opened her eyes and looked at Sheryl. The young woman wore a white peasant blouse pulled off the shoulders and a full black skirt that flared out around her as she sat in the wicker chair. "How did it go?"

Sheryl shrugged one freckled shoulder. "Okay, I guess. It was the usual assortment of females and"—she wrinkled her nose and grimaced—"one know-it-all who kept interrupting with her own wonderful ideas about raising plants. I found out later she didn't even own a cactus . . . Get out of there, Patches!"

A white cat with black and orange blotches stood on its hind legs and investigated the paper plates with a velvety nose for the source of the smell of cake crumbs. At Sheryl's sharp command the cat dropped to its feet and minced closer to Catriona.

She leaned forward and picked up a crumb to offer to the cat. Sheryl said to the animal in an indulgent tone, "You know who's the soft touch around here, don't you, you little beast!"

"Don't listen to her, Patches," Catriona soothed. "She really loves you."

Sheryl sighed and the red-gold lashes flickered down. Then she looked at Logan. "It's not me that loves that cat—it's my son, Robbie."

Catriona asked, "How is he today?"

"The same." Sheryl's hands gripped the arms of the chair. "He's an angel—he never complains." Sheryl had lost weight since Robbie's illness, and everything about her seemed more vivid, her green eyes more luminous, her skin more pale. Now those green eyes were quite openly asking her an unspoken question about Logan.

Catriona moved nervously on the couch. She sought Patches's soft fur and ran her hand over the silky cat as if it were a talisman. How was she going to handle this? She had to tell Sheryl she had agreed to go out West and work, and also that she had the money for Robbie's entrance into the hospital. If she told her about the job first, would she be less likely to link the two events? It was worth a try, even though Sheryl would undoubtedly think Catriona had lost her mind.

She took a breath and plunged. "I came to tell you good-bye." The flicker of pain that crossed the young woman's face cut deeply into her soul. "I've decided to go out West and take a job on Logan's ranch."

Sheryl's eyebrows flew up. "Doing what?"

"I'm not exactly sure," Catriona temporized. "Some—some cooking, some secretarial work"—she tried a light laugh—"maybe even some cow punching."

Sheryl was plainly incredulous and gazed at Logan's impassive face as if trying to read his thoughts. But nothing in that dark, lean face gave her a clue to the mind behind it.

"Where out West?" Sheryl asked.

"I have a ranch in Wyoming," Logan drawled, and before Sheryl could answer, a childish voice said, "What's a ranch, Mommy?"

Thin and slight in his blue T-shirt and jeans, he looked like a two-year-old, Catriona thought, her heart twisting at the sight of the little boy who was her brother's son. His red hair was tousled from sleep. In the crook of his arm he clutched his favorite sleeping companion, a kangaroo with a frayed ear. The ear was held tightly in his fingers and rubbed on his cheek.

"A ranch is a place where they raise cattle and ride horses," Sheryl said to her son. "Come here, honey, your shirt's out all the way around."

His pupils still wide from sleep, he raised round blue eyes to Catriona. "Hello, Aunt Cat," he said solemnly. "Did you come to see me?"

"Yes, I did," she said lightly. "But you were asleep."

"I was tired." He heaved a sigh and came to her. He

smelled soft and warm and his skin was smooth. But the telltale blueness around his mouth sent a shaft of pain straight through her, followed by a wild elation. In her purse was the money that would make Robbie well. "Can I sit on your lap?" he asked Catriona.

"Sure, honey, as long as your mother doesn't get jealous."

Out of the corner of her eye she could see Logan's face, and though she anticipated the usual mocking smile, it was noticeably absent. Instead, something dark and dangerous flared in those blue eyes.

"What's jealous?" Robbie ate words voraciously. He constantly asked about new ones and used others he had heard in the wrong context. He looked two and acted thirty, she thought. He had spent his time almost exclusively with grown-ups. He couldn't run or play with the energy of other children. The congenitally misformed valve of his heart barely kept him alive.

"Jealous is when somebody you love starts acting nice to somebody else."

Solemn blue eyes turned to Sheryl. "Are you jealous, Mommy?"

Sheryl, losing some of her first self-consciousness in front of Logan, dropped down on the fur rug at Catriona's feet and made a mocking growl at her. "Filled with it," she told Robbie. "How dare Aunt Cat take you away from me?" She raised one small bare foot that dangled near her and pretended to bring it to her mouth. Robbie wriggled in Catriona's arms. "Don't, Mommy."

"Okay, honey," Sheryl said, smiling up at him and letting go of his foot. "You're not quite ripe yet, anyway."

Robbie studied each adult's face in turn, ending with Logan. The three adults smiled, and Logan's face was strangely softened as he returned the boy's steady gaze.

"Do you have horses and cows on your ranch?" Robbie asked soberly.

Logan was equally serious. "Lots of them. Would you like to come and see them sometime?"

Catriona stiffened. How could Logan offer such a thing so casually and so cruelly? Robbie would talk about it for weeks.

"Yes," Robbie answered. "Can I?" This was to Sheryl.

With an anxious glance at Logan, Sheryl said, "Well, I'm not sure, Robbie. We'll have to see about that."

Robbie wiggled out of Catriona's arms and sank down on the rug beside the cat. "Can Patches come, too?"

"Patches can come, too," Logan said imperturbably, and Catriona fought down the urge to kick him.

To the cat Robbie crooned, "See, Patches, you can." Then with a tight grip under the cat's forelegs, he picked her up and began to walk toward the window.

"Robbie, please put Patches down. You know she doesn't like to be carried around."

"She doesn't care. She likes me," Robbie explained patiently.

Sheryl raked a hand through her hair and turned away from her son. "He's right, you know. That cat will let him do anything to her—almost as if she knows . . ." Her voice trailed away. Then she jumped to her feet with characteristic agility. "Mr. Blake, I've been a most inconsiderate hostess. Would you like some herbal tea? I don't keep coffee in the house—"

Catriona shot him a warning look, but he ignored it and said, "Tea is fine. Thank you."

Catriona's heart sank. Robbie sat with the cat by the window, teasing her with a cloth mouse. With Sheryl rapidly disappearing into the kitchen, she was, in effect, left alone with Logan.

Logan leaned over slightly and said with a soft, menacing tone, "I ought to wring your neck."

"Go ahead," she whispered fiercely.

"It's the boy, isn't it? There's something wrong with him . . . What is it—a problem with his heart?"

Catriona heard Sheryl's step with relief.

"I've put the kettle on," Sheryl told them. "Are you sure you wouldn't like something to eat? It is getting late . . ."

"We'll have something to eat at the club," Logan assured her.

Time was passing. She had to give Sheryl the money—and soon. "I—I've got something, Sheryl." With a degree of acting and a cool calmness she had not thought she could conjure, she opened her purse and handed Sheryl the envelope. "It's the money for Robbie's operation." Sheryl stared at her with disbelief, and she hurried on. "The bulk of the money is—is from an insurance policy I found of Dad's that—that we didn't know about," she lied. "And the rest Logan advanced from my salary." It was flimsy, very flimsy, but she could think of no other way to explain Logan's name on the bank draft. Would Sheryl accept her explanation?

"But, Catriona, I can't—"

"You must," Catriona said coolly. "It's all arranged. You simply take this to any bank and open an account. You'll have more than enough to cover the hospital costs."

"But you'll have nothing for yourself, Cat. I can't take your money."

A soft drawl startled them both. "Catriona will have her meals and living quarters provided while she's working for me. She doesn't need money to live on the ranch."

"Of course, I'll pay you back—"

Catriona shook her head. "You won't. The money is yours. Robbie is family—and so are you."

Sheryl held the check between her fingers, tears glimmering in her green eyes. "I shouldn't—but oh, Cat!"

She fell on her knees in front of Catriona and hugged

her impulsively. "How could you keep this a secret from me?"

Catriona's own eyes were bright with unshed tears. "It wasn't easy."

Sheryl got to her feet quickly and brushed at her eyes. With an apologetic glance at Logan, she said, "You'll have to forgive me. I've been so worried . . ."

"I can understand that," Logan assured her.

Joyous relief made Sheryl bubble with words. "When Con died so suddenly, I thought nothing could be worse than that. Then when we discovered Robbie had the same thing—a congenital weakness in the heart valve—I wanted to die. I couldn't bear it." She brushed away another tear. "You must realize how grateful I am to Catriona—and to you."

Logan only nodded. Sheryl went back into the kitchen and came out bearing a tray laden with the teapot and cups. She had poured a small glass of milk for Robbie. He promptly poured half into Patches's bowl.

Logan drank his tea and said little. He didn't have to. Sheryl, bubbling with relief, poured out words like a waterfall, her elation evident in the sparkle of her eyes, the quick movements of her hands as she stirred her tea. She was far too happy to question Catriona's shaky explanation of the money, and Catriona was thankful for that.

Later, singing at the club, Catriona gave vent to her own relief. Even Ken's angry glances at her could not dampen her elation. Logan sat at a table near the back, and she saw Ken searching the room with his eyes, picking Logan out of the crowd and scowling at him, but when it was time for her to sing, she forgot them both and sang with a power and feeling she had never been able to express before. Worry about Robbie had depressed her. Now, relieved of that worry, her mind and voice soared together. Each song seemed to grow and swell within her. The upturned, rapt faces of the people told her they, too, felt her joy.

It was time for her final song. Bill brushed a feathery rhythm into the waiting silence. She took a breath and began to sing the song she had written for Logan two years ago.

> I walk alone and watch the sun disappear,
> It splashes color round the bay,
> I remember what it was like to hold you near,
> But I can still hear someone say,
> Tomorrow's gonna be another day. They said,
>   "She'll get over him,
> Just don't worry about her,"
> But they don't know how much a part of me you
>   were.
> I feel like an actress,
> Putting on her show,
> So many performances, strung out in a row,
> But wherever I may be, I can hear someone say,
> You know tomorrow's gonna be another day.

After the last note died away, there was a long quiet moment. Then the applause began. It was loud and long, and she lifted her head and looked out into the darkness. In the brilliance of the spotlight, she couldn't see Logan.

A moment later, she stepped off the bandstand, and Nick caught her arm. "You were wonderful tonight, Cat. I'm going to miss you and my patrons are going to miss you." He smiled down at her. Nick was a dark-haired, smoothly handsome man in his early forties, and he was well aware of his charms. "I'd like to buy you and your friend a farewell drink." His head lifted. "You, too, Fowler."

Ken straightened from his seat at the piano, his face carefully blank. "Sorry, I've got something else to do." He strode toward the back of the stage and out of sight down the hall. Catriona watched him go, torn by guilt and a strange sense of loss. "I'll be there in a minute, Nick. I've got to talk to Ken."

Hard fingers grasped her bare upper arm. Somehow, Logan had materialized beside her from the back of the room. "Mr. Armand has asked us to have a drink with him. Your good-byes can wait till later." The words were smooth, but his grip was beginning to hurt and she knew she didn't dare risk creating a scene under Nick's curious eyes. There was nothing to do but give Logan a scathing look and turn to walk to Nick's table.

Through the thin silk of her yellow gown, Logan's touch burned. As if he had read her mind, he released her, but as they walked, she felt his hand drift to the back of her waist. They arrived at Nick's table, and just as she moved to sit down, Logan's hand brushed the top curve of her buttocks. A sharp electric shock of awareness tingled through her, followed by anger. Color warmed her cheeks when he seated her. She wished she had kicked him this afternoon. If he didn't watch himself, she would yet.

Peggy appeared from behind Nick. The club owner introduced her to Logan and held her chair out for her. When Peggy was seated, she turned brilliant green eyes to Logan.

Catriona could see Logan's appreciative male gleam returning Peggy's interested gaze. She wore a red silk blouse open in a V to the waist; the soft mounds of her breasts were visible on each side of the deftly draped material. Harem trousers tied at the knee defined the curve of her hips.

"You're from Wyoming?" Peggy asked. When Logan nodded, Peggy laughed huskily. "I feel like Columbus. I've discovered something new on the other side of the world."

Nick's smile was forced while amusement tilted Logan's lips. "Wyoming isn't quite on the other side of the world."

"As far as I'm concerned, it is." Wine was poured and Peggy sipped hers, not bothering to hide the provocative path of her eyes over the top of her glass as they played over Logan, taking in every detail of him—the lean chest visible under the suede jacket, the trim waist, the muscular legs in cream pants. She set her glass on the table and leaned back in her chair to say to Catriona, "And you're going to work for him out there?" She paused dramatically and added, "Lucky girl."

Logan smiled his slow, lazy smile. "I'm not sure Cat considers herself lucky."

"She should." Peggy turned her glass around on the table and then lifted her head to give Logan a long, intimate look.

"It is a temporary job, is it not, Catriona?" Nick asked, his voice tight with displeasure. His eyes were glittering over Peggy as he said it.

"Yes—yes, it is." She hoped the huskiness in her voice would be attributed to her singing.

"You'll be back in the fall, then," Peggy said.

"Yes—"

"Unless she decides to stay on—working for me," Logan added silkily.

Peggy lifted wide eyes to him. "Is that a possibility?"

"No," Catriona said flatly, while at the same time, Logan drawled, "I would say that it was—yes."

"You seem to have differing opinions." Peggy lifted a hand to brush a lock of hair back behind her ear, her scarlet nails vivid against the silver-blond strands. "Isn't there some cowboy song about the work being all done in the fall?"

"If there is," Logan answered her, a quirk of amusement tugging at his mouth, "it doesn't apply to my ranch. There's always work to be done, no matter what time of year it is." He slanted a mocking glance at Catriona. "If Cat turns out to be very good at the job, she might decide to stay." The full force of his smile was turned to Peggy, leaving Catriona to glare at him in helpless fury.

Peggy flashed him a brilliant smile of her own and said huskily, "I've never danced with a cowboy. Would you think me very forward if I asked you to dance, Mr. Blake?"

"Not at all." He rose politely. Peggy slid her hand into his and led him out to the dance floor.

Nick's face was livid. "The little witch," he muttered. "One of these days she is going to find she has pushed me too far—"

Thinking furiously, she said, "Why don't we dance, Nick?"

Nick's face had the dark scowl of a jealous lover. He stared at her for a long moment and then said, "Yes, why not?"

Recorded music was piped through the sound system while the band took its break. Other couples were circling on the floor, and Catriona stepped onto the smooth wood surface and turned into Nick's arms. The first circle he executed brought Logan and Peggy squarely within her vision. Scarlet nails were bright against Logan's dark nape. His hand was curved intimately into the small of her back. In the dim light Catriona met his eyes over Peggy's blond head. She forced herself to look away.

Nick was holding her stiffly, making no pretense of enjoying the dance. He turned her around and Peggy and Logan disappeared from her range of vision. They were squarely in Nick's. His hand tightened on hers and made her wince. "Nick, please. You're . . ."

Instantly he slackened his hold. "I'm sorry, Cat." The face that had been scowling suddenly beamed a dazzling smile down at her. Nick was giving her such an openly appreciative male stare that Catriona gazed back at him in amazement. Then she felt the brush of a shoulder. Logan had guided Peggy over to them.

"Shall we change partners, Armand?" Logan said smoothly. Nick feigned a reluctance, but Catriona felt his hands release her at once. There was nothing for her to do but step into Logan's arms. Peggy's angry face over Nick's shoulder came within her vision briefly and then disappeared as Nick pivoted her away.

She made a small misstep and Logan pulled her closer. For a moment he held her in the conventional way. Then he brought his hand down close to her hip and danced with her as he had two years ago. A barrage of memories swept over her until his other hand nestled into the small of her back and she remembered that moments ago it had laid just as intimately against Peggy's body. She stiffened and tried to pull away.

"Relax," he ordered softly.

A bubble of hysterical laughter came into her throat. Relax in Logan's arms—with his clean male scent filling her nose and his muscular body pressed against every inch of hers?

"Why didn't you tell me about your brother?"

The words were so incongruent she couldn't make sense of them.

"What?"

He repeated the question.

She said huskily, "It isn't something I like to talk about."

"What was wrong?"

"He—it was hereditary, something Dad's dad had, too."

"Your father died of the same thing." It was a statement, not a question, and Logan's voice was tight. "What about you?"

"I escaped because I'm female."

She felt the slight relaxation of his grip. They danced slow, turning steps, his leg moving smoothly between hers.

"Why didn't you tell me this that first night?"

She looked away from him, out across the room. Nick and Peggy were dancing closely, but their faces were dark with anger.

"Why should I have?"

A slight tensing of his body was his only answer. Then he asked, "How did it happen?"

"No one knew Con was ill. He just said he was tired one day and—collapsed. He was only twenty-nine." Simply having to talk about Con's death hurt.

"You've had a difficult time."

"There's no need to feel sorry for me," she said stiffly.

"No," he drawled slowly. "There isn't, is there?" The music ended. Logan let go of her slowly. "Get changed, Cat. We're leaving."

A sharp retort came to her lips but she stilled it. Logan was her employer and he had the right to tell her what to do from now until November.

In her dressing room minutes later she kicked off her shoes and reached around to the back to unzip the silk dress and let it fall to the floor. She wouldn't take any of the dresses with her, and somehow felt no pang at leaving her stage clothes behind. She walked to the chair in her lacy bra and panties and picked up the cream denim pants. She had stepped into them and was running the zipper up when a knock sounded on the door. "Just a minute, please."

The door swung open. She snatched up her blouse and clutched it to her breasts, a sharp word on her lips. Shock changed to surprise. "Ken!"

His eyes flickered over the creamy shoulders exposed to his gaze. She fought for composure. She had been to the beach with Ken in a bikini, but he had never walked in her dressing room like this before.

"I'm dressing," she said, her voice caught in a husky breath, her mind mocking her for saying the obvious. "Would you mind waiting . . ."

He walked toward her and the way he moved sent a small shiver of fear crawling up her spine. "Yes, I mind waiting."

His words alarmed her even more. Instinctively she moved back.

"I've been waiting for you too long already," he ground out. In one lightning move, he grabbed her by the wrist to pull her toward him.

Her Irish temper rose. He wasn't serious, he couldn't be. "Ken—stop it!"

"No, Catriona." The purr of menace in the sound of her name and the insolent focus of his eyes on her breasts told her she had been right to feel afraid.

He pulled her into his arms, the buttons of his velvet jacket pressing into her skin and his warm, moist hands on her back sending a shock of repugnance through her. The ruffles of his dress shirt felt strange under her hands as she pushed at his chest. "Ken, you can't mean this . . ."

"Can't I?" he grated harshly. "Blake had you last night—now it's my turn."

"He didn't!" Thoroughly panicked now, she was struggling wildly.

His harsh laugh echoed in the small room. "You expect me to believe that two-bit cowboy didn't make love to you?" He stilled her struggles easily. His sandy head bent and he pressed his mouth against her cheek. "For two years I've put you up on a pedestal, told myself you'd fall in love with me eventually. I thought you were the one woman in a million worth waiting for." His eyes raked over her face. "But you aren't, are you?" His voice thick with contempt, he went on. "You're not going to work for Blake—you're going to sleep with him." He held her away and stared into her face and his eyes glittered with hate—and a twisted love, she saw with sudden, chilling clarity. "Now it's my turn. I've damn well earned it . . ."

He pulled her into his arms and his lips ground down on hers. She struggled and pushed against him with her palms, her heart beating wildly, her brain unable to comprehend that the man who had been her friend was now forcing himself on her. She ached to scream but she couldn't. He was ravishing her mouth, stilling her voice, choking her. She closed her eyes, knowing that there was nothing she could do or say to stop him. When she felt his fumbling hands roam over her body, she brought her fingers up to rake her nails over his face. Suddenly the pressure from his body was lifted away.

"Get away from her!" The words were hard as steel.

She opened her eyes to see Logan's hands on Ken's shoulders. Logan pushed him against the wall and pinned him there. Shorter and slightly built, Ken was no match for his antagonist. He fought with words instead. "Let me go, you bastard," he managed to say.

Logan loosened his hold, but his eyes never left Ken. "Get out—before I change my mind about breaking your neck."

Slowly, cautiously, Logan relaxed his grip and stood away from the other man. Ken straightened away from the wall and pulled his jacket down. He glared maliciously at Logan and shot a contemptuous glance at Catriona. "I wish you luck, cowboy. You're going to need it—with her!"

"You're the one who's going to need luck, Fowler. Because if I ever see you again, I will kill you."

The words were soft but the effect was deadly. There was a long silence in the room broken only by the sound of Catriona's tortured breathing. Then, with a muttered curse, Ken turned and stalked out.

Catriona stared at the open door with shocked horror. A violent chill shuddered over her body.

"You'd better get dressed." Logan's glance moved slowly over her half-naked body but his face was dark and unreadable. He went to the door and closed it, then stooped to pick up her blouse that had fallen to the floor in her struggle with Ken and step toward her with it. Instinctively she moved away.

"For God's sake, Cat. Don't imagine you're going from one assault to another." He lifted her arm impersonally and guided her hand into the sleeve of the blouse. "I don't remember dressing a woman before, but I think I can manage it."

The touch of his hands on her body was cool and impersonal. The blouse was raised over her shoulders. Lean fingers fastened the buttons. When he began to tuck the material in under the waistband of her pants, she came to life. "I can do that."

He stepped away and pulled her jacket down from the hanger and held it out for her. "Where are your shoes?"

"Over there." He helped her slip into the jacket and then bent and held the heeled pumps for her. It seemed natural to place her hand on the broad shoulder to balance herself. "Now comb your hair and put on some lipstick," he ordered her calmly.

Like an automated doll, she obeyed again. While she brushed her hair, Logan lounged against the door and watched her. She prayed he would say nothing more.

He seemed to understand. He was silent as they walked out of the club and got into the car. But when they had turned onto the expressway that led to the airport, he asked, "Are you . . . all right?"

The soft, compassionate question made a lump rise in her throat. She fought it down and said, "Yes . . . I'm all right." She couldn't tell him that the pain she suffered was from guilt—and an acute feeling of stupidity. She had been immersed in her own misery—and blind to Ken's feelings. She had used him to buffer her mind from the pain of her love for Logan. She had never guessed Ken was emotionally involved with her.

Logan's lean hand turned the wheel of the car, and in the light from the dash she could see the dark hairs that lay above the knuckles. That hand could touch her coolly . . . or caress her to the point of madness . . . or fasten around a man's body with a killing grip. She shuddered and forced her mind away from the scene in her dressing room.

But other thoughts flooded in as she sat beside Logan, riding into the darkness. Her mind returned to the past—to the night two years ago when Logan had asked her to be his wife. They had been in the car that night, too, riding to her apartment after the job. They had been lovers for nearly a week, and she had wondered how much longer he could stay in Chicago. Out of the blue he had said it casually, as if he were asking her out to dinner. "Marry me, Catriona."

She remembered the way she had sat stunned for a moment until she realized he had really said what she thought he said and joy had bubbled through her. "Oh, yes, Logan, yes," she had answered. He had reached out to her in the darkness with that lean hand then and pulled her close. His voice had been rough with emotion. "I have to get back to the ranch right away. We'll be married there." His warm fingers closed over hers. "I want you to leave with me tomorrow."

"I . . ." All the joy drained away. "Logan—I can't. I've got to stay here and finish out this series of contracts with Con and Dad."

"Contracts can be broken," he said implacably.

She shook her head. "Not without costing money."

"You can't be the only singer in Chicago," he said dryly.

She moved restlessly in the seat. "It isn't that easy, Logan. I know all the routines, all the songs. Because we are related, our voices blend in a special way. Dad has hired a new arranger and there's even talk of our cutting a record. I can't let them down now . . . not after we've worked so hard . . ."

Logan drove in silence for a moment. Then he said, "If the record is a hit, then what?"

"Well, I suppose we'd be expected to promote it."

"Touring . . ."

"I could refuse to go on tour. We could do a short spot advertisement for television that would only take a day or so and reach just as many people. But don't you see, Logan, I just can't walk away from my family . . ."

He moved away from her. "You're the one who doesn't see. I need a wife, not a singing star."

"It would only be for a limited time . . ."

He had turned to her then, his voice hard and angry. "In the music business one success leads to another offer that can't be turned down—and another and another."

"No," she cried. "In six months I'll be free."

"Will you?" His voice was like granite. "I wonder."

She had picked up his hand and lifted it to her cheek. "Logan, please, trust me. I—love you very much."

"But do you realize what loving me means, Cat? It means changing your entire life-style—giving up all the music, the nightly excitement, the applause." He brushed her lips with his fingertips. "It's very quiet on my ranch."

"Logan, I'm not a teen-ager. I don't need a steady diet of excitement. Besides"—she turned his hand and pressed a kiss into his palm—"I'll have you."

"But will that be enough?" he asked roughly.

"Yes, Logan, more than enough." She lifted his fingers to her mouth and began to kiss them slowly, sensuously. A soft groan escaped his lips. He shuddered and pulled his hand away from her, only to wrap it around her shoulder and pull her even closer to him.

When they reached her apartment she didn't even pretend to invite him in for coffee. "Stay with me, Logan," she had pleaded.

That night he made love to her, those hands exploring every inch of her, taking her into the mysterious and wonderful realm of passion as only Logan could. Together they reached the heights and later, when Catriona lay beside him and listened to the soft sound of his breathing, she was certain that in the morning they would talk and Logan would tell her that he understood and that he would wait to marry her. They loved each other; that was the important thing, and they would work things out like two intelligent people.

When they did talk, she won Logan's reluctant agreement to go back to Wyoming alone and wait for her telephone call, but she felt vaguely disturbed the afternoon she drove him to the airport. His good-bye kiss was cool and perfunctory.

Her mind stopped there, rebelled, refused to go on and remember the rest of her agony.

She was here now, in the car with Logan, and it wasn't a dream, as it had been so many times in the past. Logan was real, alive and breathing beside her. She wanted him to touch her, kiss her, make her feel alive again . . . Oh God, she was going to go crazy if she kept thinking like this . . . kept remembering. She had to find a way to keep Logan out of her mind.

But how could she when he was sitting inches away from her, when the clean musky smell of him filled her nose and light from passing cars played over that sensual mouth? And this was only the beginning. How would she keep her mind in control for the next eight months?

His voice startled her. "Are you warm enough?"

"Yes," she said again. "How—how long will it take to fly to your ranch?"

"About four and a half hours—plus or minus fifteen minutes," he drawled. "Are you afraid to fly in a small plane?"

"No."

His next words sliced through her like a rapier. "You lied to me about the money."

She looked out the window and didn't answer.

"I'm curious. Why did you want me to think you were involved with another man?"

"That should be fairly obvious," she said huskily.

"Why bother with a fictitious lover?" he said lazily. "I know you're Fowler's exclusive property."

She turned to stare at him in the dark. "How could you possibly think that?"

He gave her question what seemed to her an oblique answer. "Your kiss the other night wasn't exactly—impersonal."

She forced herself to look away from him. "It wasn't personal, either."

"What was it?"

The question was cool and quiet, but its subtle menace played over Catriona's ears.

"Show business, Logan, strictly show business."

"Fowler didn't know it was all an act, did he?" he said lazily.

Her voice low and full of pain, she said, "Logan, please, don't."

But he went on, his voice cool and relentless. "You're very good at making a man believe you love him, aren't you?"

The urge to destroy his cool control made her say tightly, "Don't tell me I managed to fool you."

"Yes, I was fooled the first time." There was a long, heavy silence in the car. "But it won't happen again, I can promise you that," he added softly.

His voice chilled her. She stared out into the night and wished that she either loved him or hated him. It tore her apart to do both.

CHAPTER THREE

She woke from a doze. The droning sound of the airplane had made her nod off but now something about that sound had changed. Straining against her seat belt, she turned to look at Logan. His dark face was illuminated by the lights from the control panel of the plane, but he seemed to show no signs of fatigue as he prepared the plane for landing. "Did you get some sleep?" he asked.

"A little. Where—where are we?"

"Coming up on the landing strip." The plane tilted slightly. The night seemed very black, the stars close. Below, a dark, rolling land lay enfolded in the night. Here and there the blaze of vapor lamps shone, but instead of being in the orderly rows along the streets that she was accustomed to, they shone in a random pattern across the landscape.

"That's the home ranch," Logan said, nodding to the light that shone like a lonely beacon in a sea of black. "Grace and Scott live there." There was a silence and he answered her unasked question. "Grace is my stepmother and Scott is the child of her marriage to my father."

"I didn't know you had family."

His mouth moved at the corner. "No, you didn't, did you?"

He was silent then, devoting all his concentration to landing the plane.

The slight bump and the sound of rubber against the blacktop told her that they were on the ground. Logan glanced at his watch and said, "We made good time." He unbuckled his seat belt and flexed his shoulders. She averted her eyes from the movement of his body and released the metal clasp of her own belt.

He was out of his seat and undoing the safety latch on the door by the time she was free of its constraints, and she rose to follow him out of the plane. He put out the small ladder and went down, turning to hold out his hand for her. After an instant's hesitation she grasped his fingers and descended the two steps. The instant her feet touched the ground she slid her hand away from his at once.

A vapor lamp illuminated the metal roof of a small shed. Parked beside the shed was a pickup, one of the newer kinds that rode high off the ground and had oversized tires. Behind her Logan opened the hatch of the plane and collected their luggage. When he turned, suitcases in both hands, Catriona reached toward him, wordlessly asking for her bag. Though his eyes taunted her, he handed it over. Together they walked across the hard surface of the runway toward the pickup. He tossed his suitcase in the back and she did the same. Hay crackled against the bottom of the case as she set it down. Uneasily, she went to the passenger side of the pickup and climbed in. Someone had left the key in the ignition for him. Logan started the vehicle and pulled it around in a circle.

They bounced over a trail, and when Catriona thought her bones would never be the same again, Logan pulled onto a smoother path and then into a yard surrounded by a complex of buildings. She couldn't really see too much, but she did recognize the hooded shape of a barn, and the low, flat profile of a building that looked like a bunkhouse. There was a machine shed, too, and she could see the shadowed gigantic tractor sitting between the open doors.

Square patches of light gleamed out from two windows on the main floor of the two-story house into the shadows of a porch. Logan pulled up in front of the door and turned off the engine. Before she could ask whether anyone was in the house, he was out of the pickup. She had no choice but to open the door and climb down.

When she came around to the back, he handed her her suitcase matter-of-factly. He turned and led the way up to the door, his open jacket moving over his lean body, his booted feet echoing on the wooden floor of the porch. Could it be called a porch? She wasn't sure. There seemed to be columns rising to the second-story roof. The house might have belonged on a Southern plantation in Tennessee rather than in Wyoming, she thought dazedly as they stood in front of an oak door. Inside her impression of Southern hospitality was heightened. Logan strode forward into the entryway, brushing past a dark walnut antique table. A sleek modern mirror reflected his lean face. Beyond his shoulders she could see a living room done in a marvelous eclectic mix of antiques and comfortable modern furniture. Where was the knotty pine and the mounted deer heads, the fur rugs she had expected to see? Not in this civilized room, certainly. A modern velvet sofa in a striking lime green curved in front of an elegant marble fireplace. Above it a mirror soared to the ceiling. Light came from a glistening crystal chandelier.

"Your room is upstairs," he said, and started up the curving staircase. She followed, questions buzzing inside her head like a hive of bees. At the top of the stairs he paused at the open door on his right and dropped his suitcase into what she supposed was his room. She waited, keeping her eyes carefully to the front. He did not turn and look at her but went to a door on the opposite side of the hall and motioned her inside.

She got an immediate impression of miles of cream-colored carpet and cool green drapes. The furniture was gleaming golden oak, the bed large and comfortable-looking and covered by a lacy green spread. She clutched her suitcase and turned to look at him. "I thought I'd be staying in the bunkhouse."

"No," he said shortly. "None of my women employees stay in the bunkhouse."

"You have other women working for you?"

His lips lifted in a faint smile. "Not right now. During the summer busy season." Her eyebrows flew up and he drawled, "Does that surprise you?"

"Yes—yes, it does." She took a breath. "Then I won't be an oddity."

"Not because of your sex."

To her unasked question, he said slowly, "Your inexperience will make my men wonder why I hired you."

His mouth quirked and she lifted her chin. "Will that bother you?" she asked.

"No. I thought it might bother you." He leaned against the doorframe and watched her with eyes hooded with dark lashes.

"I had the impression people minded their own business out here."

He gazed at her reflectively. "To a certain extent, yes. But they also like to know what's going on. In the city people are bombarded with meaningless stimuli they learn to ignore. Country people watch everything around them because they are responsible for most of it—the animals, the land."

While she pondered that curious remark, his dark head turned as he glanced around the room. "Your quarters are satisfactory, I hope."

"More than satisfactory. But—"

A slight smile lifted his lips. "Don't think you'll be spending much time here. For right now, though, make yourself at home. There's a bathroom off this room for your private use. Take a shower and go to bed. My housekeeper will be here in the morning and you can meet her then."

"She doesn't stay here?"

Logan's eyes flickered over her. "Her husband owned a neighboring ranch. When he died, she wanted to stay on the ranch. So she came to work for me, and I run her cattle with mine with the stipulation she can stay in the house she shared with her husband."

"I see." She cast away the disturbing thought that she would be alone with Logan at night and asked, "Where will you be tomorrow?"

"Out on the range. I've been away for too long as it is. You'll be alone in the house tonight, but you're perfectly safe, believe me. Now, if you'll excuse me . . ." He dipped his dark head at her and took a step toward the door, but her voice made him pause just inside.

"You're riding out there now?"

"Yes." His eyes were cool and impersonal.

"I'm going with you."

Logan paused briefly and then shook his head. "No. You've missed a night's rest. You need some sleep—"

"No more than you," she argued. "And if I'm so inexperienced, the sooner I start, the better."

He moved his shoulders under his coat in a gesture of exasperation. "You have to be taught to ride a horse and work into it gradually."

She shook her head. "How hard can it be to ride a horse? He does all the work."

A gleam of amusement lit the blue eyes. "Does he?"

Her eyes sparkling with anger, she asked sharply, "If you had hired a man in Chicago, would you let him lie around the house for a day before he started?"

He gazed at her for a moment and then moved away from the door. "Get a shower." At the cool look she gave him, he drawled, "It will be your last one for a while. I'll meet you downstairs in ten minutes."

With a slight inclination of his dark head, he was gone. She was left staring at an empty doorway, listening to the soft drum of his boots against the carpeted hallway. When she heard the steps stop, and the two soft thumps that told her Logan had reached his room and kicked off his boots, she came to life.

The shower was warm and refreshing on her skin, and she tried not to think that Logan had meant what he said. *It will be your last one for a while.* Wanting to linger in the warm, comforting water, but not daring, she soaped her body quickly, then rinsed and stepped out to dry herself off. She wrapped the towel sarong-style around her and lifted her suitcase to the bed. She opened it and stared down at the skirts, blouses, and pantsuits. Where were the jeans and tops that Logan had bought for her? She had been so wrapped up in thinking about Robbie she hadn't thought about them. Had Logan left them in the plane? A sound of exasperation escaped her throat as she dug through the suitcase and found her robe. When she had it belted snugly around her waist, she walked purposefully to the door.

Logan had not closed the door of his bedroom, but he didn't seem to be in it, either. She stood just outside the doorway and knew she should leave, but her legs wouldn't move, and her eyes traveled over the room that she had avoided looking into only moments before. The decor was masculine, yet done with an eye to style. A thick bronze-colored carpet covered the floor and soft brown drapes curved gracefully at the windows. The bed was similar to the antiques she had seen downstairs, the headboard carved in intricate patterns of dark wood above the brown silk spread. She was admiring the fantastic view of the mountains Logan's bedroom window gave him when he opened a side door from what had to be his private bath. His mind on other things, his back to her, he was unaware of her presence, and he strode across the room in front of her with nothing but a brown towel draped around his lean hips.

She stood there dazedly staring at him, seeing the muscled shoulders moving like oiled cord under the bronze skin as he opened the door of his closet and thrust a hanger aside impatiently, the dark silky hair shower-damp at his nape, the long muscular legs covered with fine dark hair. His hand moved to the top of the towel, and the thought that he was going to strip it away made a sound bubble up from her throat. He turned at once, his brows drawn together in an angry line as if he had forgotten her presence in the house and expected her to be someone else. He stared at her and the anger and surprise were replaced by a lazy, mocking smile.

Tall, lean, and male, and utterly confident, he took a step toward her. "Did you want something?" The gleam in his eyes left her in no doubt that he had used that phrase quite intentionally.

Dry-mouthed, she said, "My clothes . . ." When he took another step and showed no sign of understanding what she meant, she took a shallow, painful breath and stammered, "The ones—you—bought."

"In my suitcase." He pointed to the unopened case at the foot of his bed.

She didn't want to open that large masculine bag to see his clothes packed with hers. "I—would you mind getting them?"

"If you were a man I hired in Chicago," he mocked softly, "I'd tell you to help yourself."

He leaned back against the wall and folded his arms as if he had all the time in the world to wait for her next move. Her body warm with anger under the terry robe, she determinedly looked away from him and walked to the suitcase. She grasped the handle and laid it on its side on the canvas-strapped caddy to snap it open. Neatly arranged on top of the masculine underwear were her jeans and T-shirts. Averting her eyes from his dark-colored briefs, she snatched the clothes up and escaped, pretending she didn't hear his soft laughter as she walked out of the room.

She was combing her hair and fastening it into braids when he stepped into her doorway. Lean and disturbing in snug jeans, a plaid shirt, and a suede vest, he held a familiar box in his hand. She could feel his eyes moving over her jeans-and-shirt-clad figure, ending with her braided hair. "Very practical," he murmured, "and workable—with the added plus of making you look about sixteen."

She ignored him and picked up the small flowered case she had packed with her toothbrush, toothpaste, and hand cream. She had also tucked in some lip gloss, thinking that it might be protection against the sun. She wished she had thought to bring suntan lotion. Her pale skin burned easily, even though she was a brunette.

"You forgot something." He held out the box with the boots. She stepped forward and snatched it out of his hands. His soft laugh irritated her even more. "The socks are inside," he said, and turned, leaving her to stare at his disappearing broad back in helpless fury.

He hadn't moved the pickup. It was still parked in front of the house when she walked out of the house toward it into a world painted with gold. Streaks of yellow splashed upward from the still-hidden sun, and a patina of pale light shimmered over earth and sky. She caught her breath. She had never seen anything like it. She stood drinking in the sight of the summer earth glowing in a tentative dawn, letting it all sink deeply into her soul—the sound of birdsong just beginning, the feel of the cool, astringent air against her face, the glorious sense of being alive.

Logan came around the pickup. Eager to share her happiness with another human being, she took a deep breath of the crisp air and said, "Logan, it's so beautiful here. I never dreamed it could be like this."

He stopped stock still. His hard blue gaze played over her illuminated face and sparkling eyes, and his mouth tightened into a hard line. Under his hat his eyes were darkly shadowed.

She refused to let his dark mood affect her and smiled at him. "I shouldn't take the time off to admire the view?"

His shoulders moved in dismissal under his vest. "I have to load our sleeping gear. Wait for me in the pickup."

"Can I help you?"

In the shadowy dawn the tight mouth relaxed into the familiar mocking smile. "I think I can handle it," was his drawled answer. Was he trying to make her feel inadequate? If he was, he wasn't going to succeed. She wouldn't let him.

Snapping up her denim jacket against the chilly air, she kept the smile pinned on her face and walked toward the pickup. The high-heeled boots felt heavy and awkward on her feet. Of course, it wasn't the boots that were awkward. It was her. Would she be able to do anything useful at all? She gritted her teeth. She couldn't let Logan's skepticism infect her thinking. Her head high, she marched to the pickup and clambered in.

In minutes, Logan had their sleeping bags and saddles loaded. He climbed in beside her, started the motor, and drove down the track they had traveled from the airstrip. But instead of taking the turnoff, Logan continued down the narrow lane and turned out on the highway.

She kept her gaze away from him and stared out the window. In the pale light she could see that the land undulated gently and was covered with a heavy thick grass that sprang away from the earth in sharp angles.

"What mountain range is that?"

"The Bighorns," Logan told her and volunteered no more.

"How far are we going?"

"The men should be close—maybe only about fifty miles away."

"That's close?"

He made a sound of amusement deep in his throat. "Out here, it is."

She gave up her attempt to make polite conversation. Logan seemed lost in his thoughts, and she supposed he was thinking about the work that lay ahead of him.

An hour later they drove into the camp, and the rising sun cast a reddish-gold glow over the dark figures of men, horses, and cattle. Several of the ranch hands, the collars of their denim jackets turned up, were huddled at the back of another pickup as they drank coffee and ate their breakfast. Others were seated on rough benches under a tent awning while they ate. Two men leaned against the tent pole, their legs crossed, holding their flat-bottomed coffee cups. Their eyes lifted to the pickup as Logan braked it to a halt.

He got out and went around to the back. She did the same and was getting ready to help him unload their sleeping bags and saddles when a man's voice said, "Good to have you back, Boss." The man who walked toward them was older—perhaps in his late forties—and had the short and stocky body of a cowboy whose work on the range had carved itself into every muscle. "Did you bring back a new ranch hand?" Under the broad-brimmed hat his eyes were amused and curious.

"Catriona Morgan, Seth Davis. Seth is my foreman."

Catriona put out her hand, and Seth whipped off the sweat-stained Stetson and his glove and clasped her cold fingers. His grip was firm, his hand lined with calluses that rasped against her palm. His face looked as rough in the early morning light as his skin felt. If there were questions on his mind about her presence in the camp, his friendly, natural greeting didn't show it. She liked him at once.

"Find many late calves yesterday?" Logan's voice was crisp and businesslike.

As if startled by the brusqueness of Logan's voice, Seth Davis dropped Catriona's hand and gave his boss a sharp look. "Three. They all came through okay."

"Catriona can ride with Jim and Noah. They can sweep behind and look for strays and mothers with new calves. Charlie almost done serving?"

Seth Davis settled his Stetson back on his head and grinned. "Yeah. Want me to tell Jim to get a horse for you?"

"I'll do it," Logan told him and walked away.

Seth chuckled and glanced at her. "Want to see something real pretty?"

Puzzled, Catriona nodded.

"Then come and watch Logan cut out a horse."

She had no choice but to follow Seth Davis across the rough earth to a temporary corral. Inside, horses, their coats ranging in color from a pale cream to a dark burnished brown, were circling close to the fence in an effort to escape Logan.

"He's after that roan mare for you," Seth Davis told her.

The rope coiled in his gloved hand, Logan stood silently, waiting for the herd to break. They quivered and tensed, but didn't move. Then suddenly, with a pounding of hooves, they whirled and ran to regroup behind him, their ears laid back, their bodies taut. For a mere instant the roan was in the open. Logan's hand moved and the rope snaked out. With a downward flick of his wrist Logan dropped the rope neatly over the roan's head.

The horse knew the game was over. She stood quietly, quivering silently under the rope that Logan had pulled taut.

Logan repeated the procedure with a horse Seth told her was a black Arab gelding. In what seemed like far too little time Logan had saddled both horses and was leading the roan toward her. The horse tossed her pale mane with a restless impatience as if she knew she were being put into the hands of an inexperienced rider while the gelding blew through his nose as if sympathizing with the mare.

Seth put his hand to his hat. "Well, if you'll excuse me, ma'am, I'll be getting back to work."

Catriona watched him walk away and wished he wouldn't go and leave her alone with Logan.

"This is Lady," Logan said softly, leading the horse up to Catriona. "She's gentle but she knows about cows. She's trained to neck rein so try not to confuse her by letting the reins touch both sides of her neck at the same time."

Catriona moved around to the outside of the horse and Logan made an impatient sound. "What are you doing?"

"Getting on."

"Not from that side, you're not," he contradicted her harshly. "You mount a horse from the left—always. Here, take the bridle and talk to Lady. And for God's sake, don't let her know you're frightened."

Incensed, Catriona said truthfully, "I'm not afraid of her." Keeping her voice low, she added, "I don't particularly like being yelled at, that's all."

"Would you rather I let you try and mount up on the wrong side and get tossed to the ground?"

She didn't reply. His softly mocking words made her more determined than ever to get into the saddle—and stay there.

She stroked the horse and murmured to her. The horse blew into her palm and sidestepped nervously. Catriona was glad that what she had said was true. She had always loved animals. But this horse was larger than she had imagined somehow. "All right," she whispered fiercely to Logan. "Now what?"

"Put your left foot in the stirrup and swing yourself into the saddle," he instructed tersely.

With a quick glance around the camp to assure herself that the men were busy rolling up bedrolls and getting their own horses saddled, she lifted her foot and slid it into the stirrup. She balanced herself precariously and swung her other foot over the saddle. Miraculously, she was up, sitting on the back of the horse, the reins in her hands. Lady sidestepped nervously and blew again as if in protest, and instinctively Catriona put her hand out to pat the horse's neck.

"There is a pair of gloves in the pocket of that jacket. Get them on. Where's your hat?"

"I left it in the pickup."

Logan cursed softly and turned on his heel. She sat quietly, trying to get used to the unaccustomed spread of her legs over the saddle and the feeling of being farther off the ground than she cared to be, and watched him jerk open the door of the truck and pull her hat from the seat.

From a few steps away he tossed it at her. Luckily, she caught it. "Keep track of your personal belongings," he warned her, his voice commanding. "A good ranch hand doesn't slow the rest of the crew down."

She muttered a harsh word that wasn't ladylike and glared at the man who lifted himself into the saddle with the easy grace of long practice. Then she raised the hat and jammed it on her head. The remains of coffee cups were being dumped on the ground and saddles were thrown over the backs of horses. There was a general movement out of the camp, but, far from being frisky or cantankerous, Lady simply wouldn't move. Helplessly, Catriona watched as Logan rode away with the other men. She spoke to Lady in a cajoling tone, trying to get her to move.

Lady stood her ground. With the exception of the camp cook who was washing pans with a great rattle and bang, Catriona was the only person left in the camp.

Then, as if her distress had called him back, one of the younger men wheeled his horse around. When he saw she wasn't moving, he urged his horse toward her across the lush green grass.

He pulled up beside her and asked politely, "Are you having trouble?"

His smile was friendly, and to Catriona he was straw to a drowning woman.

"This horse won't move." Her tone was so plaintive that the cowboy laughed.

"Kick her a bit," he instructed, lowering himself at once in Catriona's opinion. She couldn't see herself kicking the mare.

"I don't want to do that."

"You'd better," he told her unfeelingly, a laugh in his voice, "or you'll still be sitting here when we come back. Come on, Lady—move."

He made a clucking sound with his tongue, and Catriona, driven by desperation, lifted her feet and brought her heels down against the horse's sides. Lady took a hesitant step forward and then another and another. She began to trot at last, and Catriona was jounced uncomfortably up and down in the saddle. Her companion reined his horse in beside her and shot her a surprised look. "You haven't ridden much, have you?"

Catriona shook her head ruefully. "Does it show?"

"A little," he said kindly. "Look, try and squeeze your legs together and let them take more of your weight. If you don't—well, you're going to be pretty sore at the end of the day," he finished tactfully. "Keep your heels down. You'll have more control."

"Thanks—"

"Jim." He supplied his name for her. "Jim Hardin."

"I'm Catriona Morgan."

When she told him her name, he grinned at her. "How come you're working as a ranch hand when—" He reddened suddenly and closed his mouth.

She smiled, liking him again. "When I can't ride? I'll tell you about it sometime. It's a long story."

"I'd like to hear it, but"—he glanced up—"not now."

She lifted her eyes and saw that Logan had halted and was turned in the saddle, watching them. He controlled the restless movements of the huge black horse under him with a careless ease that Catriona could only watch with deep envy.

"Problem?" His gaze sliced over Jim Hardin.

Hardin cast a nervous glance at Catriona and then shook his head. "Nothing serious."

"I couldn't find the right button to push to get this darn horse going," Catriona said, half laughing at herself.

"Ride on ahead, Hardin. Tell Seth I'll be with him in a minute."

"Yes, sir," Jim answered, and with one kick of his foot put the horse into a gallop that took him quickly away.

"Don't start anything with him, Cat."

The low warning wiped every trace of amusement from her face and brought her chin up sharply. "I hadn't intended to," she shot back.

"No?" The word was drawn out, cool and insulting.

"No," she denied firmly, shaking her head.

"There isn't a woman born who can resist testing her charms on an eager young man," he grated.

Goaded by the unjustness of his accusation, she said hotly, "You're an arrogant, prejudiced"—she groped for a word that was bad enough and finally sputtered inadequately—"male! You shove all women into one catagory and think you have everything all figured out, don't you?"

"I won't have you causing trouble among my men."

Furious that he was determined to see her in the same

light no matter what she said or did, she retaliated. "You hired me, Logan. You can't stop me from being with your men or talking to them or smiling at them, can you?"

His eyes blazed over her. Under his powerful thighs his horse moved restlessly, as if sensing the tension in his rider's muscles. Then his face smoothed into a cool blankness. "Don't say you weren't warned."

"Is that a threat?" she asked, her voice heavy with false sweetness.

"Yes," he said huskily. He glared at her for another long moment. Then one quick movement of his forearm and the horse turned eagerly, ready to release his nervous energy by galloping away. Logan left her without looking back. Her cheeks hot with anger, she leaned forward to urge the roan into a gallop, and then clung to the saddle with every muscle in her legs as the horse responded to her urging and raced over the grass.

Jim motioned her into place between himself and an older man, whose face under his soft gray hat was even more lined than Seth Davis's. She managed to guide the mare to the general area of Jim's waving arm. They were driving the cattle out of a makeshift corral onto the open range. She could feel Lady's muscles working smoothly under her. Like a red tide, the herd moved slowly ahead. Jim rode closer and shouted, "Try to keep the back ones from breaking away. Let Lady have her head. She knows how to keep a steer from breaking loose. Noah and I will cover the sides."

She nodded to show that she understood—and she did. She just didn't know how to do it. She had all she could do to stay on the back of the horse.

Even through the thick grass, the dust rose up to fill her nose and coat her face. Her lips dried and felt painful, as if they were going to crack. The terrain was not level, but rolled forward under Lady's feet and then up again. She was glad she wasn't susceptible to motion sickness. Then the real work began. The downward pull of gravity seemed to encourage a steer to break away. One would race off to the side of a hill and Lady would tear off after the escaping cow to edge it back into the herd, Catriona clinging to her back.

The sun climbed higher in the sky. Jim and Noah shed their heavy jackets and tied them to the back of their saddles. She would have done the same, but she hadn't a clue as to how to go about it. Instead, she tugged at the gripper snaps and let the breeze blow over her perspiring neck.

What had begun as a lark became an endurance contest with her mind. She broke the never-ending ride into small segments. *Stay in the saddle until you ride up that hill. Just ride the horse down that one. Now ride to the top of this hill.* The words drummed in her mind until they broke into a steady litany. A kind of numbed agony locked her muscles into an upright position.

From the general noise of bawling cattle and drumming hooves, she heard the sound of horse's hooves close by. "Little Bighorn Creek isn't too far from here," Jim called to her.

"Now I know the truth. Custer wasn't really killed in battle, he was battered to death riding over this countryside."

He laughed. "Hey, don't give up now. You're doing great. Just hang in there. We'll be breaking for lunch in another hour."

She groaned softly. Was that supposed to make her feel better?

She twisted in the saddle and tried to locate Noah, but he had disappeared.

"Jim, where's Noah?"

"Looking for a stray he saw run into a sheltered place near some rocks. He thinks she's got a calf stashed away there."

Before Jim had finished explaining, Noah appeared at the top of a rise with a calf sprawled over his saddle. The white face was alert, the ears lifted. The young calf's hooves dangled down along Noah's side and ended just at his knee. Behind him a cow bawled.

"He's beautiful," Catriona breathed. "Isn't he?"

"Yes." Jim grinned. "His mama's not too happy though. She looks a mite angry."

Carefully, Noah rode closer to the herd. Just on the outside, he swung out of the saddle and lowered the calf to the ground. The youngster tottered on wobbly legs over to its mother.

Noah rubbed a hand over his mouth and looked up at Jim. "Lucky that youngster had an experienced mother. A young heifer calving for the first time might have gone off and left him there. And I'd be danged if we'd ever have found him tucked back in the rocks like that."

The calf was nuzzling his mother, looking for the source of his nourishment. "Looks like he's a determined young 'un. He'll be all right."

Noah tilted his hat up with a pointed forefinger. His bright brown eyes swung toward Catriona and Jim. "Well, are you two gonna sit there and gape at a nursing calf all day or are you gonna work for your dinner?"

Jim grinned. "We figure you're doin' such a good job you don't need us getting in your way."

The old man made a sound in his throat and spat on the ground. "So you're gonna let an old man do all the work?"

Jim laughed and Catriona let a smile lift her dust-covered lips.

"Do we have any choice?" Jim asked, smiling.

Catriona's smile faded. Jim's teasing question reminded her that she was the one who had no choice at all.

She thought her nose was permanently filled with dust. At Little Bighorn Creek the cattle fanned out and waded into the shallow stream. The chuck wagon truck was set up in the shade of a cottonwood tree and the smell of cooking beef filled the air. Several of the men got wearily off their horses and sprawled face forward in the grass for their noontime rest.

Catriona reined Lady in next to Jim's gray and ordered her shaking legs to propel her out of the saddle. Nothing happened. She groaned. "I can't get off this horse."

Jim chuckled. "Need some help?" He dismounted easily and came around to her.

"I'm afraid I won't be able to stand up once I do get down."

"Chivalry is not dead," he said, grasping her by the waist and lifting her up and away from the saddle and down into his arms. His hands didn't leave her waist when he saw that her shaking legs refused to support her. She tightened her grip on his upper arms and tried to support herself. Trembling, half laughing at herself, she smiled up at him. "I thought the horse did all the work."

"Typical greenhorn thought." He smiled down at her. "One thing about greenhorns—they tend to learn fast." His hands were warm and comforting around her waist. He held her easily, supporting her but not holding her tightly.

From somewhere behind them Logan said with soft menace, "Maybe it depends on what they're being taught."

CHAPTER FOUR

Logan's voice sliced between them. Jim turned to face him, his arm still around her waist, his face reflecting a kind of nervous defiance.

"She's had a rough morning," he said defensively.

Logan's eyes narrowed. "She knew what she was doing when she made the decision to work for me."

Jim's face reddened. "How could she when she didn't even know how to ride?" he shot back.

Logan turned to gaze at Catriona with narrowed eyes. "You've confided in him?"

Jim said angrily, "She didn't tell me anything. She didn't have to. It's obvious how inexperienced she is . . ."

Logan looked at Catriona's dusty face and then said, "But not in everything."

The ordeal of the morning and her own fatigue as well as the injustice of Logan's accusation made a wild fury well up inside her. "You have no right to say that."

"Don't I?" The drawl was purposely suggestive.

Jim looked from Catriona's angry face to Logan's taut one. "Catriona—"

"Why don't you go take a rest, Hardin?" The words were casual, but the tone was not.

It was an order, and Jim knew it. Still, he hesitated, but Catriona put her hand on his arm. "Don't, Jim. This doesn't involve you—really."

With a sound of disgust the young cowboy turned and strode away toward the grassy spot under the trees where several of the men had sprawled on the ground to rest.

Catriona moved to follow him, but a hard hand on her upper arm stopped her. "Take your hand off me," she told Logan in a chilly voice.

"I warned you to leave him alone."

"He was helping me off my horse," she replied, her voice barely controlled. "If you keep on, you'll put ideas in his head that weren't there to begin with."

"A man only has to look at you to get ideas."

She tilted her head and her eyes glittered with challenge. "Yes, I'm especially well turned out today," she taunted. "My makeup is a new shade of Wyoming brown everyone's simply dying to try, and my cologne is a specially blended fragrance courtesy of your cows. I'm at my most seductive."

The cold anger faded from his eyes. His lips lifted in amusement. "Yes, I can see that."

"Now, if you don't mind, I'd like to join the rest of your help under the shade of that tree. I can certainly understand why they are all lying facedown," she said ruefully, rubbing her posterior. She brushed past Logan and began to limp away, only to feel the amazing grip of Logan's hand under her elbow, helping her.

She lay down on the soft grass and forgot Logan, forgot everything. After nights of insomnia in Chicago she curled up and slept like a child. Noah's hand on her shoulder brought her awake, and after a lunch of roast beef and potatoes and a delicious slice of fresh sourdough bread she forced herself to climb back into the saddle. The afternoon was hot and dusty and the cattle were more sluggish. They clearly did not want to move, and Catriona shared their sentiments. She was quite sure she would never sit down comfortably again.

The afternoon wore on to a hot and dusty end. They crisscrossed the creek, flushing out stragglers and finding new mothers with their calves.

By the end of the day she was sure there wasn't a bone left in her body that hadn't been twisted, a muscle that hadn't been pulled beyond normal torsion.

They camped close to the water and someone lit a fire. She had washed her face and hands in the bucket of warm water the cook had provided, and tried to act appreciative when she was handed a plate of food, but after a few bites she decided she needed sleep more than food. She returned her plate to the bench near the pickup and wandered back to the fire, drinking the black, strong coffee.

The trucks came with the horses and supplies and left again, and she watched them go wistfully. Out here those signs of civilization seemed out of place, unreal. Most of the range was fenced, of course, but there still was so much open space! She set her cup down and wandered away from the camp toward a cottonwood tree. The leaves rustled in the soft breeze. In the west the sun was setting, turning the sky to a deep velvet rose. *This is the first time in my life I've ever seen a sunrise and a sunset in the same day,* she thought with astonishment. She watched the rose color grow deeper and turn even the clouds over her head a pale pink.

Behind her, near the fire, someone was strumming a guitar. She turned to see that Jim was sitting on the ground, his legs crossed, his head of chestnut-colored hair bent over a guitar. His fingers moved agilely over the strings and he was singing softly. Not a cowboy tune, but a strangely haunting version of "Evergreen."

She hesitated, thinking of Logan's warning. Forget him,

her mind said defiantly. The music was calling her with an irresistible tug, and she forced her abused legs to carry her over to the circle of the firelight.

"Nice," she said when he had finished. "Where did you learn to sing like that?"

Jim smiled up at her. "I'd like to say it comes naturally, but actually my parents paid for several years of expensive lessons. Do you like music?"

"A little," she admitted cautiously. "What else do you know?"

He mentioned some songs that had been standard in her repertoire.

Jim patted the ground. "Sit down."

Catriona groaned. "Must I?"

Jim laughed. "Here. Use my jacket for a pillow."

When she had settled herself gingerly on the ground, he launched into a song that she particularly liked. She sang along, and when the song was over, he turned to look at her. "Hey, you're really good. You could be a professional. Have you ever thought about a singing career?"

"My father was a musician," she said, hedging. "He was one of those self-taught types. He could pick up almost any instrument and play it. My brother was the same."

"Are they—"

She told him about the destruction of her family in a few brief words.

"I'm sorry," he said softly. "It must have been hard for you."

"What about you? What are your plans for the future?"

He shrugged. "I'm not sure. I suppose I'll end up in computer technology somewhere, but it's hard to give up the idea of ranching. Once you get used to the life-style it gets in your blood." His fingers strummed softly over the guitar strings. "My parents can't understand why I do it. I tell them it was all their fault. They sent me out here when I was fourteen to stay on a dude ranch one summer, and after that I just had to keep coming back. In the city it seems as if everybody is angry about something or other, but out here"—he grinned self-consciously—"it's hard to nurse a grudge against your fellow man when you can see miles of land and acres of sky just by turning your head." He paused and glanced at Catriona. "Are you from Chicago?"

"I've lived in quite a few places, but I guess you could say I'm from Chicago."

"That's where you met Logan?"

"Yes." She dropped her eyes and plucked at a blade of grass. The camp fire flared suddenly.

"Is there something between you two? Is that why he's warning me off?" Jim stared into the fire's glow.

"It's not what you're thinking—"

"The regular hands have been wondering about those frequent trips to Chicago."

She looked up, startled. "They had nothing to do with me."

"Didn't they?" Jim's voice took on a harsher tone that contrasted with the soft music he was playing. "The stockyards in Chicago are closed. There's no reason for a rancher to go there anymore."

"I don't know anything about his activities."

"It's none of my business, anyway. All I know is that he's never watched any of the other women he's had working on the ranch like he watches you." A sudden hard chord sounded in the air. "He's giving me a complex."

Jim stared across the fire, and Catriona turned to follow his gaze. The firelight played over Logan's face as he stood on the other side, drinking coffee. Under the broad-brimmed hat his eyes were hidden, but he was facing in their direction and she knew he was staring at them.

Jim strummed a final cadence on his guitar and got to his feet. "I'm turning in."

He walked away toward the horse corral. She felt cold

and alone suddenly and she wanted to call him back but she couldn't. She couldn't let him become entangled in her struggle with Logan. Jim was right to object to Logan's constant supervision of their conversations, but there was nothing either of them could do about it. He was their employer.

Seth Davis, sitting near the fire, shifted uncomfortably as if he felt the tension. *The regular hands have been wondering about those frequent trips to Chicago.* Did they all believe she was Logan's current lover?

The thought was intolerable. She had hoped to become less conspicuous as she learned to ride and do her fair share of the work. Now it seemed she would be denied even that. She felt an urgent need to get up and get away. She started to scramble to her feet, forgetting her aching muscles, and gasped as they reminded her of the ordeal she had forced them to endure. She supported herself with her hand and, gritting her teeth, pushed herself upright.

A few awkward steps took her out of the light of the fire and into the shadowy sanctuary of the trees. She put out a hand to lean against the trunk of a cottonwood and stood staring out into the night. Above the dark shapes of the rolling hills stars glittered, more than she had ever seen in her life.

The sound of booted feet against the earth came from behind her. She knew that rhythmic step.

"Something wrong?" Logan's voice was soft, yet achingly familiar.

She didn't turn. Instead, she took a breath and said, "Yes."

"Want to tell me about it?"

She faced him, her features lit by the dim light of the fire while he was nothing but a shadowy silhouette. "Your men think I'm having an affair with you."

A slight shrug lifted his shoulders. "Does that bother you?"

"Yes, it bothers me. I want you to leave me alone."

"I'm responsible for your safety."

Savage anger flooded her. "My safety?" Her voice was low and intense with contempt. "When have you ever cared whether I lived or died?"

"When you accepted the offer of my employment," he said softly, his own voice carrying a hint of steel, "you made me responsible for you."

"You weren't much concerned about me two years ago."

"I wasn't aware that my lovemaking was hazardous to your health," he said softly, his tone amused.

Thoroughly, painfully angry, she grated between clenched teeth, "Not to my health but certainly to my—"

She clamped her mouth together, but he finished it softly, "Emotions?" He took a step closer and she backed away instinctively, brushing against the tree. "Were your emotions involved, Catriona?"

"No—"

"You're lying," he said softly, advancing on her, his body as supple as a tiger's while hers was stiff with fatigue and tension.

"Don't—" She took another step back and an exposed tree root caught the heel of her boot. When she stumbled and lost her balance, his arms shot out to catch her. He held her steady, his hands hard on her upper arms. Fatigue stripped away her defenses. Her body reacted to his touch like a drug addict to the drug long denied.

She was so close to him that she could see the hard glitter of his eyes, smell the warm, musky scent of his body. "I swore I wouldn't touch you out here," he muttered huskily, and for a long moment he held her away, the muscles in his arms strained with the effort.

She stared into his dark face in the breathless silence, no longer caring that their absence after this length of time would be noticed at the campfire. She only knew what every feminine instinct was telling her—that he was as disturbed as she was. That had never happened before. In the past when he made love to her, he had always been coolly in control, orchestrating his responses to match her own. Now, she could feel his arousal, the pounding of his heart against her palms. A sudden wild elation filled her. She was consumed by a primitive urge to take him to the limits of his control and beyond, to shatter that hard hold he had on himself. Slowly, purposely, she insinuated a questing finger in the bare spot below his neckerchief and traced along his flesh down the open neckline of his shirt, raking the hair-covered skin lightly with her fingernail. "Sir Galahad," she mocked softly. "I never would have suspected it."

His hands tightened and his eyes burned down into hers. For a breathless moment his hands were iron clamps on her arms. Then a low growl of disgust came from his throat and he pushed her away. "You little witch!" he said softly, almost conversationally, watching her as she clutched the tree and tried to regain her equilibrium. "You're lucky I've had more experience than young Hardin, or you'd be wondering how to stop me from taking what you offer so freely."

He pivoted and strode away, leaving her to clutch at the tree trunk and swallow convulsively in an effort to contain the sick revulsion that filled her throat . . . not for Logan. For herself.

If he slept close to camp that night, she wasn't aware of it. Tucked in her sleeping bag, she expected to lie awake for hours on the hard ground. But physical exhaustion took its toll, and she closed her eyes and was asleep almost at once.

A hand on her shoulder woke her. She opened her eyes to a world that was dark and cold, and completely alien.

"Better get up if you want some chow," Noah's sandpaper voice said in her ear. "Charlie don't wait for nobody."

She moaned and tried to move. Every nerve registered pain.

"Won't be bad once you get up and get moving," Noah assured her. "Here. The boss wanted you to take this jacket. He thought you might need it this morning. It's a little heavier than yours." He stood up and lifted his head to the wind as if scenting the temperature. "Turned off a mite cool last night."

She wanted to tell Noah what the boss could do with his overworked sense of responsibility and his jacket. It was Logan's, of course, lined with sheepskin. But when she sat up and unzipped her sleeping bag, the nippy air made her reach for it. "Thanks, Noah. How I can brush my teeth?"

Noah's lined face crinkled in a grin. "There's fresh water in the milk can by the chuck truck."

After a wash in the creek and a hurried brushing of her teeth, she felt marginally ready to face the day. A quick glance over the heads of the men gathered around eating breakfast and drinking coffee in the light of the hanging lanterns told her that Logan's tall figure was not among them. Relaxing slightly, she forced her legs to carry her over to the pickup, where a white-aproned Charlie was dishing steaming hot food onto tin plates.

Charlie's sourdough biscuits were unbelievably light and tasty. The coffee was hot and steaming and there was strawberry preserves for the biscuits, along with eggs, bacon, and fried potatoes for those with hearty appetites. To her own amused chagrin, she ate everything on her plate.

The second day was a monotonous repetition of the first. She had a different mount, a dark bay gelding, but as if the long hours in the saddle the day before had given her a concentrated short course in horseback riding, she knew that she was handling the horse better and that they were working more as a team than she and Lady had done. Noah kept up a running stream of patter about the cantankerous nature of cows in general, the vagaries of the weather in particular, and the injustice in the poor lot of a cowhand. Catriona was glad for his tirade. On the other side of her Jim rode quietly and seemed to be greatly interested in any part of the landscape that she wasn't in. When they stopped for lunch, there was still no sign of Logan. She had sprawled next to Noah on the grass, and now she put her plate aside and said casually, "Where's Logan? I—I should give him back his jacket."

Noah squinted at her from under the battered gray felt hat. "He rode on ahead to get a branding corral ready." Then a sly grin split his face. "You and the boss getting along okay?"

"Fine," she lied, "no problem."

Noah leaned back on his hands and squinted up at the cloudless sky. "Been working for Logan since he took over for his pa." He paused. "Thought he'd get married years ago," he said, chuckling. Catriona tensed. She did not want to hear about Logan's past affairs, but she didn't see any way of stopping Noah's recital without betraying her own emotional involvement. He continued relentlessly. "That McClain woman almost had him, but she tried to get him to sell the ranch and move to the city. He didn't cotton to that. He ain't about to let a woman tell him how to live his life." His shrewd gaze played over her face, which she had carefully molded into lines of polite interest. "Seems like sparks fly when you two look at each other." He gazed at her, a shrewd amusement glimmering in his eyes.

"Logan and I don't always agree on a lot of things. We're very different people."

He mused softly, "Yeah—male and female." He let that succinct observation sink in and then said, " 'Course it all could be my 'magination . . ."

"I'm sure that's what it is," she agreed, keeping her tone casual and giving up the hopeless task of convincing him that he was wrong.

She had the feeling she hadn't fooled him. He said nothing more when it came time to mount up, but throughout the afternoon, as she moved more easily in the saddle and worked with an intense concentration to keep the cattle in her small sphere moving, she felt his young-old eyes swing to her dust-stained face more than once.

By evening she felt as if she had always ridden a horse behind red-coated cattle, that she had always felt dusty and sore and tired, and that she had never sat in a hot tub of clean water. If she were ever allowed that incredible luxury again, she would savor every moment of it.

After a very unsatisfactory wash in a pan of water provided for that purpose, she ate supper and dropped into her sleeping bag to fall into an immediate deep sleep.

When she woke in the dark the next morning, she crawled out of her sleeping bag to her feet with slightly less difficulty than she had before. Her muscles seemed looser, not as stiff. They were becoming accustomed to the exercise, she thought, or was it the warmer temperature? The air against her face was not nearly as cold as it had been the morning before.

After she washed, she went to the chuck wagon truck and collected a plate full of food. Carrying her steaming hot cup of coffee in one hand and her plate of biscuits and eggs in the other, she walked to a boulder and sat down. Instinctively she turned to face the rising sun, and was glad she had left her jacket open to the soft early morning breeze. The sky was a gold and red symphony played against a background of blue. This was Logan's country—his way of life. He had come back here, after meeting her in Chicago—and forgotten her.

Automatically she began eating, but her thoughts were far away. She remembered how she had felt, watching

Logan walk down the boarding ramp and climb in the plane to fly back to Wyoming and away from her. She had been able to let him go only because she was sure that in six months she would be flying to him.

She had not counted on the success of the record album. Her father had, after years of trying, succeeded in making that one-in-a-thousand hit record. Offers poured in. They were even asked to play a week's run at the prestigious Rainbow Room in Chicago. Through the excitement she kept in touch with Logan by telephone. When the six months were up and it was evident she would be needed to make personal appearances for another two months to take advantage of the feverish success of the new record before its popularity died away, Logan became annoyed and angry. They had had a long-distance argument that lasted an hour.

She had been caught between a cold, adamant Logan, and a brother and father riding high on the euphoric success they had hungered for so long.

Then one night Logan refused to take her call. The next day she had gone to Conrad and told him she was going to Wyoming for a few days. He had been furious.

"You can't, Cat. We have a concert scheduled and two benefits."

"All right then, I'll make the trip in twenty-four hours. Please, Con, I've got to see him."

"Yeah, and when you come back you'll be too beat to sing."

But she had gone in spite of Conrad's objections. When she called Logan from the Sheridan airport and begged him to come and see her, he had agreed—until she told him she could only stay for a few hours.

"It's no use, Cat. It won't work. It was never right for us. You have your life and I have mine."

"Logan, please, you've got to listen to me . . ."

"Get on the plane and go back to the city. That's where you belong—not on a ranch in the middle of Wyoming."

Desperately, she had cried, "Logan, we love each other. I want to live my life with you."

"Honey, let's not kid ourselves. You've lived without me very well for the last six months, and I've managed to survive without you. We had an affair and now it's over. Let's not prolong the agony."

She had argued with him, pleaded with him, but nothing she said made a difference. In the end they had said good-bye like two polite strangers. She hung up the phone with a numb coldness born of the knowledge that he had never really loved her.

She had to face it. He couldn't have felt anything for her and turn her away like this. Perhaps he had merely asked her to marry him out of compassion. She had told him often enough that she loved him. Perhaps he had only felt sorry for her. The thought made her shudder.

In the small airport she stood motionless, feeling a numbness that lasted only momentarily. Then her knees trembled and her eyes filled with tears, and she could hardly see as she fumbled in her purse for her return ticket.

Somehow she boarded the plane and returned to her life and her work, but the woman who returned from Wyoming was not the one who had flown there.

Seven months later her father had died and Conrad had followed. Catriona had been devastated. The life that had been so bright and full of promise was suddenly meaningless . . . and on top of her grief she felt guilty—guilty for resenting the family ties that had prevented her from becoming Logan's wife.

She had forced herself to pick up the pieces and go on. Sheryl had needed her and so had Robbie.

Robbie. He was the reason she was here in Wyoming now. Well, she supposed she had work to do. Reluctantly, she slid off the rock and picked up her plate and cup. She had to show Logan that she could handle whatever work he gave her. But hard on the heels of that thought came a whisper in her mind that she would have to do that for the next seven months and twenty-seven days and hide her love for Logan during every minute of it.

The sun climbed higher and beat down on her head. She had lost her hat somehow during the last two days, and she hadn't the faintest idea where it was. Her hair was no longer braided; it hung loose around her shoulders. She knew her nose would be a fine shade of red after today, if it wasn't already.

The clatter of cups and silverware into the enamel pan that Charlie kept ready signaled that breakfast was over and the workday beginning. Catriona deposited her cup, plate, and utensils in their designated place.

"You got a feisty one this morning," Noah told her when she went to the corral to pick up her horse. "Think you can handle him?"

Her mount was a gray gelding and there was something about the horse's eyes Catriona didn't like. He seemed docile enough standing there with Noah's hard hand on his bridle, but his ears flickered nervously. "Is he—does he buck?"

"Naw," Noah scoffed, "he don't buck. But he might decide to take you around in a circle just to see if you're paying attention."

She eyed the gray with misgivings. "Why can't I have the horse I rode yesterday?"

Noah grinned. "Horses rest, people don't." He put a hand out and stroked the gray muzzle. "Smokey's all right, he's just got a little inferiority complex, don't you, Smokey old pal? His brother was a racehorse and got shipped off to Nevada and ol' Smokey thinks he should have gone, too."

Catriona laughed. "Now, Noah, I know I'm from the city but I'm not that gullible."

The jeep that bounced into the campsite distracted Noah momentarily. His eyes narrowed and he studied the swirling dust raised by the wheels for a moment before he turned back to Catriona, shrugging his narrow shoulders. "Okay," he rasped, "don't say I didn't warn you. Horses got feelings, too, you know." He squinted sideways at the gray. "Want me to top him off for you?"

At her puzzled look he explained patiently. "I'll ride him first an' let him get the friskiness out of his system."

The driver of the jeep levered himself to the ground, and Catriona's pulses leaped as if prodded by an electric wire. It was Logan, dark-jawed, his eyes heavy with fatigue, his mouth hard. He glanced in her direction and then headed for the horse corral.

She was still in his peripheral vision, however, and if Noah rode the gray and then handed the horse over to her, Logan would see every minute of it. She shook her head. "If I'm going to spend the day with this darn horse, he'd better learn who's boss."

Noah nodded. "Saddle him up and he's all yours."

She hoped it wasn't her imagination that this horse was able to hold his breath longer than any of the others she had saddled. At last he gave in. The gray sides collapsed and she pulled the belt into place quickly and fastened it. "Okay, Smokey," she muttered under her breath as she gathered the reins and prepared to mount, "you make one false move and you've had it."

"You've become very Westernized, talking to your horse."

Logan's lazy drawl came from somewhere over her shoulder and caught her just as she was ready to mount, one foot off the ground. She fought to regain her balance and leaned against the horse to turn and find Logan behind her, his eyes half hidden under dark lashes, the brim of his hat shadowing his face. In his gloved hands he held the reins of a black horse standing obediently beside him.

"It makes a pleasant change," she said coolly. "He can't talk back."

Logan cast a quick glance over the restless gray. "Don't be too sure. Horses have their own way of communicating with people." He was quiet for a moment and under his hard gaze she shifted nervously. "Did you have any paticular instructions for me today?" she asked.

"No, just keep doing what you've been doing."

She nodded. He was too close, too male. She moved back a step and turned to mount the gray. Her motions were quick and caught the gray unprepared. The horse sidestepped and whinnied. Logan's horse nickered a low, answering warning. Startled, the gray bobbed its head, making the reins jingle. Somehow Catriona was up and in the saddle, but the gray's nervous jittering made her uneasy.

"Who gave you this horse?" Logan asked sharply, and reached for the reins.

Before she could answer, the gray took offense to Logan's reaching hand and danced away. "Damn it, Cat, get down," Logan grated.

She couldn't risk it. What if the horse reared and trampled Logan? She gave Logan a warning look and tried to keep a semblance of control over the skittish horse.

"Get down from that horse," Logan ordered sharply. "Now!" He reached for the reins again, and though he was quick the horse was quicker. His head bobbing frantically, he gave a snort and whirled to escape.

She heard her name in a hoarse shout and then everything seemed to blur in front of her. The gray gathered his powerful legs under him and ran at breakneck speed over the open prairie on pounding hooves, his mane fluttering against her hands, his ears back. She could only cling to the reins and pray that when she fell she wouldn't catch her foot in the stirrup and be dragged to her death.

The wind whipped past her face. She gritted her teeth and tried to pull on the reins but it was useless. She felt so helpless, and she was terrified.

She must be hallucinating. The sound of pounding hooves seemed to grow louder and double in intensity. Then out of the corner of her eye she saw Logan riding next to her, the black's knees lifting, his neck straining to pull alongside the gray. Oh, God, he wasn't going to try to pull her off, was he? He was a cowboy, not a stunt man in the movies. He would be killed . . .

"Kick out of the stirrups and let go of the saddle," he shouted, and there was such command in his voice that the moment she felt his arm around her waist she did exactly as he had told her.

There was a horrible moment when they were locked together, the horses banging into each other as they pounded forward side by side. When she was sure they were riding to their death, his hand tightened painfully around her waist, and she was dragged across the saddle and clamped next to his side. Desperately, she clung to him, trying to get a grip on his shirt or anything that would ease the drag of her weight on him. His iron grip showed no sign of loosening. Locked to his side, she rode with him until he tugged on the reins of the black and the horse slowed in response. The gray, free of his burden, was running diagonally away from them.

Logan pulled the black to a halt and loosened his grip on her. Deeply thankful to be alive, Catriona slid to the ground next to the panting horse and wondered if her unsteady legs would support her. She managed to stay on her feet and totter a few steps away so that Logan could dismount.

He swung out of the saddle, every muscle in his body tight with fury. His face dark and taut, he took the step that brought him directly in front of her. "You damn little fool! Why didn't you get down off that horse when I told you to?"

Catriona was stung and her own temper flared. "Because a damn big fool was in the way and if that horse had reared . . ." She stuttered to a halt and stared at him in silent fury.

He went very still. His eyes played over her dust-streaked face. Then he murmured, "You were thinking about me? I find that hard to believe."

She stared at him and the knowledge that he had put the worst possible interpretation on her actions came crashing into her brain. No matter what she did, he would always think her motives were perverse. Trembling in reaction to her thoughts and the wild ride, her eyes filled with sudden tears. She twisted away and stared out over the open prairie, the green grass and purple hills blurring in her vision. "Think what you like," she told him, her tone bitter. "You will anyway."

"Catriona." Her name was a low, husky plea, but she didn't turn. Hard hands dragged her back against him. Then she was being turned into his arms. She focused her gaze on his red kerchief, but a finger under her chin lifted her unwilling eyes to his. "You are a little fool, you know." She stiffened and he smiled. "But I was a bigger one—for thinking I could ever stay away from you . . ."

He bent his head and her anger intensified, welled up inside her and threatened to choke her. She couldn't bear to have his mouth on hers, not now, not after he had shown her how little she meant to him. He thought of her as enticing female and nothing more, and it wasn't enough. It hadn't been enough two years ago and it wasn't enough now. Repelled, she put her palms against his chest and pushed. "No, Logan, don't."

His lips brushed her temple. "Don't?" His husky, amused tone made her anger flare white-hot.

"Let me go!" she whispered fiercely.

His answer was to fold her even closer into his arms. "You don't mean that . . ."

She lifted her foot and aimed a kick just above the protective covering of his boot. Leather cracked against bone, and he cursed and slackened his hold. "What in hell—"

She stepped backward, staring at him, her breathing quick and disturbed. "I told you to let me go," she said, her voice low and furious.

"You pack a kick like a mule," he rasped, rubbing the sore spot on his shin. "Next time I'll let you stay on the damn horse till you fall off and break your neck."

"You do that, Mr. Blake," she shot back. "I'd much prefer it to your stunt-man tactics."

He muttered a curse. His mouth tightened and his eyes glittered that deep cobalt blue that was a sure sign of his controlled fury. He dipped his head and tugged the brim of his hat down. His tone coldly sardonic, he countered, "Then I won't make the mistake of offering you a ride back into camp, Ms. Morgan."

He reined the black around, vaulted into the saddle, and turned his horse to ride away before she realized that he intended to leave her alone on the prairie—a good half mile from the campsite.

She cried out his name but it was too late. The horse was galloping away across the green grass with Logan's ramrod straight figure on its back.

CHAPTER FIVE

The sun beat down on her head and the walk back was hot and dusty. She rehearsed angry speeches to deliver to Logan along every step of the way, but when she got to camp, he was nowhere to be seen.

"Coward!" She had her head down and was muttering under her breath when she walked around the chuck wagon and ran head-on into Noah.

His hands caught her. "You all right?" he asked, his concern making his sandpaper voice rise a tone higher.

"Dandy," she replied.

"Miz Morgan, I'm mighty sorry I handed you that peck of trouble."

Suddenly aware that he was feeling more than a little guilty, she put her hand on his arm. "Don't worry about it, Noah. I'm the one who is to blame. I thought I could handle that stupid horse."

"The boss sent Jim out to pick him up. Couldn't do it himself for fear he'd kill the critter, I reckon." The old cowboy peered at her from under the dusty felt hat. "You didn't tell the boss that I was the one who gave you ole Smokey to ride, did you?" Noah asked, his face worried.

She shook her head. "Why would I do that? You warned me he was frisky," she said, shrugging. "Don't worry. Nothing happened."

But something had happened. She had seen how hopeless her love for Logan was. Determinedly thrusting that thought to the back of her mind, she took her customary place behind the herd. Cattle and crew were moving slowly toward the branding site that Noah told her Logan had set up in the north corral.

When she mounted the sorrel mare without a moment's hesitation, Noah gave a soft grunt of approval.

As they rode along, she could see he was struggling to contain his thoughts. He lost his struggle and edged his horse closer to hers. "You believe in getting right back on the horse, eh?" he said, smiling, a look of guarded relief in his eyes.

"Isn't that the tradition in the West?" she shot back, not wanting to tell Noah she was too angry to be afraid.

"For a city girl you seem to know a lot about us."

"Well, you don't suffer from lack of publicity, you know. Any magazine you pick up these days has something in it about the West, the struggle for land, the way this kind of life"—she waved her hand toward the herd ahead of them—"might die away. Everyone has this romantic image of the strong, silent cowboy—man and his horse against the elements and all that."

Noah chuckled as they rode companionably along. "Sure beats me how a dusty, dirty job behind a bunch of cantankerous cows got to be ro-mantic."

She shifted her weight in the saddle. "On the other hand, I couldn't see you getting in your car every morning and commuting through the rush-hour traffic to work, Noah."

The old man laughed, a deep, raucous sound. "No, sir, you sure wouldn't see me doing that. I don't even like to go to town much."

"I rest my case," she said, smiling.

Her anger melted away. Why was it that Noah could accept her for what she was and even tease her about it? They were worlds apart—he was an old range hand and she a young woman from the city—but their common bond of understanding had grown steadily since they worked and rode the range together. Why hadn't that happened with Logan? Why couldn't she break through the misconception he had about her?

On the other hand, why should she try? She was here to work, nothing more. She had to forget the love she had felt for Logan; it would never be returned . . .

"See those trees?" Noah waved a hand to the east, and on the horizon were the shapes of trees strung along in a curving line of what was probably a creek—ash and box elder and cottonwood, newly green with spring leaves. "Those trees mean we're heading close to home." He gazed at them, his eyes narrowed against the sun. "I always did think they were the prettiest sight."

The herd, smelling water, surged forward, and they were soon within the shelter of Noah's trees. Catriona lifted the heavy weight of her hair away from her heated nape and fantasized about a rest in their shade. The familiar numbness in her rear, that most abused part of her body, told her that it was nearly noon.

When they rode into camp, the odors from Charlie's cook stove tantalized her nose. Out on the range lunch was "dinner" and it was worthy of the name. Hot potatoes, slabs of roast beef, corn, sourdough biscuits, and a delicious chocolate cake washed down with gallons of coffee made the meal a hearty one.

After she had eaten an amount of food she would never have dreamed of consuming in the city, she lay down to take a short rest on the grass under the trees with the rest of the crew. She was just beginning to relax when, much too soon, on some unspoken signal she never seemed to catch, the men woke, stretched, and went back to their work. The crew started the branding, and Catriona wandered over to the corner of the corral to watch. Jim and another young cowhand roped a spindly-legged, white-faced calf and brought him to the branding crew. Another man heated the long-handled iron over a butane torch and burned the Double B brand—two Bs, one slightly offset from the other—into the flank of the unfortunate animal. The smell of burned hair and hide combined with the medicinal dip sickened her and Catriona turned her head away. But when the calf was freed, he ran past her with no sign of pain, stretched his neck in a protesting bawl, and began to search the herd for the scent of his mother.

She felt uneasy. She was useless to the branding crew. She couldn't rope calves and she wouldn't have offered to wield the branding iron. She wandered to the creek and watched it bubble over the rocks. The sudden wild thought came that she needed a bath desperately and here was clear, clean water. For one heady moment she considered it. Then common sense prevailed. It was broad daylight and there was no way she could strip off her clothes and bathe in that shallow stream without being seen. It was only inches deep and the tall trees provided no protection at all. The idea of a full bath was out. But she could certainly go wading.

With the first real lift of spirit she had had in days, she sat down on the grass and pulled off her boots and socks. She wrinkled her nose at the dusty state of her feet and rolled her jeans up as far as she could, just above the knee.

At the bank she hesitated. Were there poisonous snakes in Wyoming? She supposed there were. She eyed the tall cattails on the other side of the stream warily. She hoped there were't any in the immediate vicinity.

She peered into the water. It bubbled over the flat brown rocks, every one of them clearly visible. How deliciously cool the water looked and how good it would feel on her warm feet! She gathered her courage and stepped cautiously forward onto the slippery top of a submerged rock. The cool water washed over her foot and she laughed with delight. Unhesitatingly, she walked into the stream, stepping from one flat rock to the other.

She couldn't recall water ever giving her such sensual pleasure. She reveled in it, picking up her feet and slapping them down, shivering from the delicious shock of cold water splashing up on her hot, bare legs.

"Hey! Who gave you the afternoon off?"

She looked up to see Jim standing on the bank of the stream, a grin splitting his face. His hat was off, a sure sign that he wasn't working, and he was grinning broadly at her, but he held his hand in front of him in an odd way.

She smiled back at him. "Doesn't look like you're working very hard at the moment, either." The trees dappled shade over his head, but there was definitely something strange about his stance. "What's wrong?"

"Calf kicked me," he said shortly. "Caught me in the wrist. I'll be all right in a minute."

She waded toward him. "Come and put it in the water. The coolness will ease the pain."

"Are you sure, Florence Nightingale?" he mocked.

"Well, it can't hurt," she said sharply. "If you don't clean the wound, you could get an infection. Here, I'll help you take off your boots."

He shook his head self-consciously, but she persisted. After pulling and tugging, she managed to get them off. He hastily withdrew his foot when he saw that she was going to peel off his socks and roll up his jeans and did the task himself with his good hand.

"Now, let me help you." She grasped him by the elbow and urged him forward. He was embarrassed by her attentions, she could see, but sheepishly pleased too, and he followed her into the water despite his obvious reluctance.

When they were ankle deep in the stream side by side,

she turned to him. "Well, what are you waiting for? Get that hand in the water."

"Yes, ma'am," he mocked and stooped to do her bidding.

She knelt beside him and gently turned his wrist over to look at it under the water. The gash was a curving one and the flesh had started to discolor around it. "Doesn't it feel better?"

"My hand's too cold for me to tell." His voice had a strangled sound, as if he were trying to keep from laughing, and his eyes glittered with amusement.

Was it the stoic code of the cowboy to be amused over an injury, she wondered curiously? "Can you move it?" She leaned over slightly to get a better look.

"I'm not sure. Let me try." And in one quick motion, he cupped his fingers and whipped water straight up into her downturned face.

She sputtered helplessly. When she could see again, she cried, "Why you ungrateful—" Her palms shot out and with one quick shove she pushed him backward. He fell off his haunches and sat down with a resounding splash.

At the look of surprise and disbelief on his face, she laughed aloud. "Two can play that game, Mr. Hardin."

He stared at her for a moment and then lunged forward. Instinctively she reached out to ward him off, but her reaching hands grasped his shoulders, and instead of helping her, his momentum carried them both down into the water, his body sprawled heavily over hers.

"Jim," she gasped, laughing, the breath half knocked out of her by the impact of their fall. "Jim, get up!"

He looked down into her laughing face for a long moment. The teasing amusement in his glance faded and the warm look of a man for a woman he desires flared in his hazel eyes. His hand under her nape lifted her toward him, and he pressed his mouth against hers in a hard kiss.

"Hardin!"

Logan's harsh voice made Jim's reaction instantaneous. The heavy weight on her body was lifted at once and Jim hoisted himself to his feet. He stood looking nervously at Logan, and Catriona sat in the water looking at him, watching the red creep to the tips of his ears. Then, as if he just remembered her, Jim turned and held out his hand. She shook her head and said blandly, "That's the one you hurt, remember?"

Sheepishly, he offered her the other one. She grasped it and heaved herself out of the water.

"So this is your new ranch hand." The feminine voice was husky and slightly mocking.

Catriona's eyes had been fastened on Logan's lean figure, and she hadn't noticed the woman standing beside him. Now she saw that his companion was a woman, a woman dressed in a green silk blouse and snug jeans tucked into her riding boots . . . a woman who managed to look both feminine and completely natural in her Western clothes.

In her water-soaked shirt and jeans and the grime of three days on the range, Catriona rubbed her palms down the sides of her thighs and began to step gingerly over the rocks and out of the water. Jim followed.

Logan's companion said something to him in a low tone and laughed, but Logan did not laugh with her.

In response Jim muttered a soft, biting word, and though Catriona didn't catch exactly what he said, she guessed at its meaning and concurred.

"Why aren't you over with the branding crew, Hardin?"

Catriona said quickly, "He's been hurt—"

Logan interrupted harshly, "But not so badly he can't play in the water with you."

Catriona glared up at him and wished she had her boots on at least. She felt like a hissing kitten taking on a big sleek tiger. "He was kicked in the wrist."

Jim put a dripping wet hand on her arm. "You don't have to fight my battles." He faced Logan, his body stiff with tension. "Seth told me to take a break and I came over to see what Catriona was doing. I told her I had been hurt and she was concerned about me. She told me to soak my hand in the water. She reminded me so much of my mother that I splashed water in her face and from there on"—he made a gesture with his hand—"it just sort of escalated."

There was a silence. From the distance Catriona could hear the shouts of the men working with the cattle, and overhead the cottonwoods seemed to rustle in sympathy. A sudden breeze carried the scent of the red-haired woman's perfume to her nose, and Catriona felt as if that fragrance had come from another world that was only a dim memory.

"Is it possible that you are well enough to resume working?" Logan gazed at Jim, his eyes shadowed under the cream Stetson.

"Yes—sure." Jim snatched up his boots and stockings, and after a quick, apologetic glance at Catriona walked away, wincing as his bare feet came down on an occasional pebble.

The woman's eyes traveled over Catriona's dirt-streaked face and down her wet shirt and jeans. "Aren't you going to introduce me, Logan?"

"Catriona Morgan, Diana McClain," Logan drawled.

"Logan tells me you're from Chicago, Ms. Morgan. What brings you out to Wyoming?"

"I wanted some fresh air," Catriona said sweetly, fighting to control her temper, her mind working furiously. This must be the woman Noah had told her about, the woman Logan had wanted to marry.

"Are you finding that behind Logan's cattle?"

Catriona smiled faintly, hiding the tight control she had on her temper. "Oh, absolutely. The drive has been delightful." She paused and then said casually, "Actually I'm enjoying myself. I suppose you are so used to this gorgeous country you take it all for granted."

Diana McClain gave her a cool look. "I'm well aware of the beauty of Wyoming," she said shortly. "I was raised here." She turned to Logan, her head high. "I'll wait for you over by the horses while you finish talking to Ms. Morgan. I'm sure there are some things you want to say to her." She walked away, her tall body moving easily over the grass.

Logan turned slightly to watch her go, an amused smile lifting his lips. When Diana McClain was out of earshot, he turned back to Catriona.

She forestalled him. "Are there some things you want to say to me?"

His mouth quirked. "Who told you about Diana?"

She lifted a shoulder. "What difference does it make?"

"It makes a difference to Diana. I suggest you keep your tongue guarded with her in the future."

She faced him with her head high, her back straight, her dark hair beginning to dry and move in the breeze. "Is that a direct order from my employer?"

His eyes held hers for a moment and then they dropped, traveling over her, insolently gazing at the way her wet clothes clung to her breasts and hips. A mocking smile curved his lips. He ignored her challenging words. "You'd better get your boots on before you catch cold."

She bridled, like a cat stroked the wrong way. "Your concern for my health is extremely touching."

"It should be," he said silkily. "If I weren't worried about you catching pneumonia, I'd never voluntarily suggest you put those weapons back on your feet."

A gleam of wicked amusement made her blue eyes sparkle. "Does your shin still hurt?"

He met her glittering look with a slight smile. "I'll live." A lazy amusement played over his lips. "Maybe I should take advantage of your shoeless state and finish what I started this morning."

"I wouldn't try it if I were you," she said, her voice husky. "You might find I have other weapons."

He tilted his head slightly. "You weren't fighting Hardin."

"I would never need to fight Jim. He—"

"I can see my technique is all wrong," he interrupted smoothly. "I should have told you your kick crippled me for life and played on your sympathy the way Hardin did."

She thought of Diana. "I wouldn't feel sorry for you if you were lying on your deathbed."

His lean body tightened as if she had physically struck him. "No, you wouldn't, would you." His eyes glittered a dark cobalt blue with a sudden fury.

He turned a broad back to her, and she stared at that denim shirt stretched across hard muscles and was unable to believe she had actually made him angry.

That night she lay in her sleeping bag and thoughts of Logan kept her from sleeping. She tossed until after midnight. She could see the flickering light of the campfire behind her and the dark shapes of the other men lying on the ground. She had just turned over restlessly for the fifth time when in the distance she heard the first low rumble of thunder. A male voice said something in a low tone.

Swiftly, the thought came to her that they were exposed to the elements, and a sudden rain would soak them all. She vaguely remembered a yellow slicker that Logan had thrown in the pickup.

The thunder came again, louder and closer this time. She huddled down into the sleeping bag and someone swore, making her smile at his vehemence. A cow bawled as if in sympathy. The thunder grew in volume and there were groans and rustling all around her. The men were getting to their feet. Then a hard hand grasped her shoulder. "Get up," Logan ordered. "We'll take shelter in the pickup."

She would have protested, but she saw that the other men were rising and rolling up their sleeping bags. She did as Logan had ordered, kneeling on the ground, the bag clumsy in her numb fingers. The night air was chilled with the coming rain. Logan let her fumble with the heavy material for a minute and then took it away from her and finished rolling it into a neat bundle. She scrambled around to find her boots and sat down to push them on her feet. When she had finished, Logan tucked her sleeping bag under his arm and held out his hand to her. He was faceless, a dark form outlined against the dying fire. Wordlessly, she grasped his hand and let him pull her to her feet.

He guided her across to the pickup and opened the door. She climbed in and sat shivering while Logan went around to the other side.

He was tucking the sleeping bag in behind the seat when she asked, "What about the other men?"

"There are enough trucks for everybody to crawl in somewhere."

He sat well away from her, leaning his long frame back against the opposite corner of the cab. His voice was cold and remote. She shivered, her body and mind chilled by his physical and mental withdrawal.

"Here," he said in a harsh voice. "Take my jacket. And stop worrying. Hardin will be all right."

The heavy weight of the suede and sheepskin jacket tossed on her was almost as much of a shock as his assumption that she was worried about Jim. Struggling with the weight of both, she shook her head. "I can't take your jacket. You keep it. I'll be all right."

She thrust his jacket back at him. With a sound of exasperation he took the jacket back and laid it across his lap while he swung his arm over the back of the seat and retrieved her sleeping bag. With a flick of his wrist he untied the strings. "Here. Put this around you. I'd run the motor, but I can't do that all night and God only knows how long this storm will last."

He unzipped the bag completely and tucked the edges around her, his hands wedging under her body with a cold, impersonal briskness. She fought down her response to his hands, to being alone with him in the closed confines of the cab, and laid her head back against the seat in what she was sure would be a futile attempt to sleep. She heard Logan moving, trying to get comfortable. Could he do that—just fall asleep with her sitting next to him? Within a few minutes his deep, even breathing told her he had done just that.

Relentlessly, her mind played back over the events of the day. Did he really believe she cared for Jim? He must have and he was angry because she had disrupted his work crew. She sighed. She would have to discourage Jim's attentions. She had to find a way to retain her position on Logan's ranch. She was fond of Jim, but nothing serious could ever come of their relationship. She had made a bargain with Logan and she would see it through and then return to Chicago . . . Her eyes closed.

A crack like a gunshot jolted her awake. Thunder boomed and rain beat down on the windshield. What was happening? Where was she? Then lightning lit the sky and she saw everything, the rolling landscape, the cattle bumping each other restlessly in the corral, as brilliantly as if it were day, and she remembered.

A streak of lightning sizzled to earth and the thunder followed almost at once. A soft, involuntary noise bubbled from her throat and Logan stirred.

"What's the matter?" His voice was husky and slurred with sleep.

"Nothing," she lied, her voice ending in a nervous little laugh. "I just—the thunder startled me."

The soft slide of cloth told her that Logan had straightened in the seat. He lifted his arms and pressed his hands against the steering wheel in a constricted effort to stretch. Then his lean body relaxed. "Are you frightened?"

The temptation to lie was strong, but something about the intimacy of the dark night and the soft, listening intentness radiating from Logan made her admit the truth. "Yes. I've been afraid of thunderstorms since I was a kid."

There was a silence, and almost as if he had said it, she could see him trying to picture her as a frightened little girl, hiding under the bedclothes. "What did you do then? Run to your mother?"

She shook her head. "No. There was only my father and Con, and they thought I was stupid and silly to be afraid of loud noises."

Hard hands grasped her and she was pulled toward him and tucked in under his arm before she could protest. His hand pressed her head against his chest. She knew that he had reached for her out of sympathy for that little girl of long ago, but she breathed in his warm male scent and felt the steady pounding of his heart under her ear and the sensations that swept over her had nothing to do with childhood.

The sleeping bag was over both of them now, and it seemed natural to slip her fingers across his waist and nestle them just above his belt between his upper arm and his side.

Another crack of lightning made her jump. His hand gripped her tighter. "You're all right, honey."

Rain beat a pattern on the metal roof over their heads. She was locked in Logan's arms in a world closed in by the drumming sound and the warmth of his body underneath her and the sleeping bag over her. His steady breathing made his chest rise and fall under her ear, and unbidden came the memory of the first night they had made love.

He had begun to caress her, tenderly at first, and then as she gasped with a reaction she couldn't conceal, he had taken her to a height of passion she had not believed could exist between a man and a woman.

A harsh splitting of the sky and its thunderous retort brought her back to the present. Like the gray clouds above that were hidden in the darkness, a depression settled over her. Nothing had changed. Logan had awakened in her an insatiable need that would never be assuaged by another man. He was the man she loved, and would always love.

Logan's breathing changed subtly and took on a shallow, restrained quality that told her he was not unaware of her feminine form pressed against him. "Logan." She whispered his name softly in the darkness, not even certain why she felt compelled to feel it on her lips, when suddenly he grasped her and hauled her into his lap. She lay across him, pressed against his chest, trapped by his arms. The lapels of his jacket cut into the softness of her breasts. When she made a strangled sound of displeasure, one quick motion of his shoulders shrugged the jacket away. Lean, muscular arms enfolded her and the dark shadow of his head bent toward her. His mouth closed over hers, warm and strangely tender, as if he were kissing that little girl of long ago, soothing her hurts, driving away her fears. All thought of resistance fled. She met his kiss with her own mouth pliant and eager, and when he would have drawn away, she sent her tongue into his mouth, probing and exploring the warm, moist depths. A shudder of desire racked his body. His hands tightened and then loosened, his fingers drifting around to the rise of her breast. He brushed her feminine peak enticingly, and then with one swift movement tugged her blouse apart. The small popping sounds of the snaps filled the silence. She made a muted sound of protest, which died at the touch of his hand on her bare back. The sudden coolness told her her bra had been loosened. Strap and blouse were pushed off her shoulder together, and then she was lying in his arms, her half-naked body a pale ivory form in the darkness.

He supported her back and turned her away so that the thrusting fullness of her breasts was easily accessible to him. Cool air touched her and with it came a measure of sanity. But even as she thought of resistance, she knew she was powerless to stop him—and even more powerless to deny herself. She had ached for his lovemaking far too long to deny her clamoring senses now. Every cell of her body told her that reality was better than memories—oh, so much better! She was going to have another night to remember. She wanted it, needed it! His fingers found her breast and explored the sensitive tip with a delicate touch as if she were made of the finest silk. A sharp tingle of pleasure coursed through her. Her hunger for him welled up within her and she was lost. She gasped and clung to him, inviting him—begging him—to continue. His fingers teased and caressed, while his mouth touched her closed eyes with light kisses. He drew away slightly, and a flash of lightning illuminated his face. Hard, glittering desire glowed in his eyes. He wanted her as desperately as she wanted him. Then the light was gone, and she was plunged back into the sensual world of darkness where his mouth trailed a warm, tingling path down her throat toward the rounded flesh that swelled to fill his caressing hand.

She tilted her head back in silent acquiesence to his feathery kisses. His hair brushed her naked skin and his mouth tantalized her with its leisurely path downward. The rosy peak of her breast ached in anticipation. When at last his lips settled over her and his tongue began its erotic discovery of her nipple, the ache deep within made her arch her back and moan, offering all of herself in sweet sacrifice to his mouth. Her hand sought his bare flesh, and when she had succeeded in finding the taut skin of his back, she grasped at the smooth muscle and buried her fingernails in him, claiming him for her own. His rasp of breath rewarded her. He acknowledged her ownership and marked out his own on her flesh, burying his head between her breasts, kissing the smooth, flat valley, then letting his tongue travel to her other breast to favor it with his sensual attention.

Once again he turned her, this time to lay her on the warmth of the sleeping bag and follow her down on the seat, his weight heavy on her. His hand went to the waist of her jeans, and he breathed her name in a low, husky sound. She raised her hands to clasp his face in loving supplication, and the thunder rumbled—and kept on in a rhythmic pattern that did not stop.

Logan cursed softly. He brought the sleeping bag up and covered her before he sat up and rolled down the window. She heard his harshly angry voice saying, "What is it?"

"There's a break in that temporary corral fence, Boss." Noah's voice sounded strained, and in the light of the battery lantern he carried his face looked even more strained. "A few critters broke through and more are itchin' to do the same." He cleared his throat and then said roughly, "Seth thought you'd want to know."

"Go back and help him and I'll be there in a minute." Logan rolled up the window and Noah swung away, carrying the light.

"Catriona . . ."

She huddled in the corner. Cold logic had replaced heated desire. "Just go," she whispered.

Outside an exasperated shout tore the air. Logan cursed softly, grasped his jacket, and got out of the cab, closing the door so quietly that it was somehow a stronger indication of his anger than slamming it would have been.

Her hands shook as she refastened her blouse. The blood beat heavily in her veins, and her heated flesh seemed to burn. Outside the storm had begun to abate.

The lightning was less frequent and the thunder only rumbled in the distance. But the storm of emotion inside her whirled on even as she swathed herself in the sleeping bag and laid her head back against the seat.

She awoke to a sparkling clear morning. As if to remind her cruelly of the night she had nearly spent in Logan's arms, her body felt cramped in every muscle. She opened the door and climbed out of the cab and down onto the damp ground. Dazed by the brilliance of the sun, she stood and looked around. The camp was nearly deserted. The men had moved the cattle on, and even the chuck wagon truck was gone. The breeze rattled the papery leaves of the cottonwood together, and that was the only sound she heard. She had been abandoned. She took a step out from the pickup and saw that there was another car parked close to the trail that led to the branding site. The car horn sounded and a feminine figure stepped away from the car and waved her hand back and forth in a wide arc.

After a moment's hesitation Catriona headed in the direction of the car. Her muscles protested at the sudden demand for movement, but she continued along the trail that was spotted with occasional puddles.

The woman stood by the car and watched her approach. When Catriona was close enough really to see her, she saw that the woman was about her own height, with silver hair done up stylishly in a chignon at the top of her head. She wore a jacket of peacock blue with a divided skirt. A bright yellow scarf tucked in the open collar of her jacket fluttered attractively in the breeze. Catriona gazed at her and felt even more grubby and unkempt. The woman appeared not to notice and greeted her enthusiastically, her eyes bright. "Hello. Did you think everyone had left you?"

Catriona saw now that the woman was older than she had first thought her to be. There were fine lines around her eyes and throat that made her think the woman might be somewhere in her early fifties. "Yes. Yes, I did."

"Logan asked me to come and take you back to the house. He wanted you to have a chance to sleep. You had a difficult night, I understand."

For a moment she was nonplused. Then she knew her vivacious rescuer was referring to the rainstorm. "Yes."

"Well, come along and get in the car. I'm sure you're dying for a bath."

Catriona faltered momentarily and the woman gave her a quick, sympathetic look. "I'm sorry. Logan didn't tell you I was coming to collect you, did he? I'm Grace Blake." Mrs. Blake opened the door of the silver-gray small-model car. "Come on, get in. I'm to take you up to the house and introduce you to Marian so she won't throw you out, and then you're to have a bath and rest for the remainder of the day. Logan's orders."

She should have argued, but she simply didn't have the strength, and the idea of a bath was far too attractive to refuse.

When they had both climbed in, and Grace Blake had maneuvered the little car around, she settled back and said conversationally, "Well, how did you like your first cattle drive?"

"I—it was interesting."

Grace Blake threw her head back and laughed. "I can't remember ever thinking that. Those first few years I went out with my husband, I pronounced it dirty and boring. And I'd been raised on a ranch."

"Well, perhaps that's why."

Grace Blake flicked a glance at her and said, "You're from Chicago, Logan said."

"Yes."

Catriona waited for the next obvious question—what are you doing in Wyoming?—which didn't come.

"Logan has instructed me not to ask you any personal questions," she said candidly.

Catriona smiled. This woman's honesty was like a fresh wind blowing across her tired mind. "What is it you don't want to know?"

The woman paused briefly and then said, "When Logan talks about you, I detect a strong note of personal interest."

She hadn't expected that. "Do you?" she said huskily. "I'm sure you must be mistaken."

The woman shook her head. "I don't think so. I've known Logan for a good many years and he's been acting strange for the last two. And it all dates directly from a trip he took to Chicago—where you live," she finished softly.

"I—I think you must be mistaken."

"Well, never mind. You're here now and that's the important thing."

CHAPTER SIX

She sat in the bathtub and luxuriated in the warm water. Aching muscles relaxed as she reveled in the silky feeling of moisture against her skin. She tilted her head back to rest on the cool porcelain and sank low into the water, submerging her shoulders, feeling the slight buoyancy the water gave her legs. She wanted to let sensual pleasure seep into every corner of her mind but she couldn't. Grace Blake's words rolled around inside her head, along with the knowledge that she had nearly let Logan make love to her last night. Let him! She had encouraged him, enticed him, aroused him. It was little wonder he thought she was a woman who made love easily and freely to every man she met. He couldn't know that he was the only man who had ever torn away all her carefully erected defenses and aroused her to a fevered passion she couldn't control.

She soaped her arms and then raised a leg to give it the same treatment. She was caught in an intolerable situation. She was committed to spending most of the year here on Logan's ranch. If she was to survive the next few months, she would have to find a way to treat him with the cool deference of an employee to an employer.

A small voice in her mind laughed derisively. *You're dreaming. He touches you and you melt.*

Then I'll have to make sure he doesn't touch me, she answered the voice fiercely.

Her pleasure in bathing vanished. She stood up and pulled the fluffy towel from the towel rack. She couldn't let Logan use her again, she just couldn't. Another affair with him would destroy her.

The thought weighed heavily on her mind while she dressed in the clean jeans and snug T-shirt Logan had bought for her. The idea of wearing cowboy boots was not appealing. She dug in the closet and found a pair of sneakers she had brought with her.

After blow-drying her hair and tying its black, silky length back with a blue ribbon that matched her shirt, she went out of her room and down the stairs.

The pungent odor of warm raisins, freshly baked bread, and hot coffee met her nose and drew her toward the kitchen. Grace Blake had introduced her briefly to the housekeeper, but the older woman had given Catriona a quick, uninterested look and gone back to work. Now, Catriona hesitated outside the swinging door. There was nothing else she could do, she argued silently. Grace had said Logan's instructions were to rest. She couldn't do that. And she didn't want to wander back out to the branding site. The only other alternative was to offer her services in the kitchen. She braced herself and pushed the door open.

"Hello," she said, trying to greet the housekeeper easily. Marian Carter stood in front of a large flour-covered board, making a pie crust. "What's that delicious smell?"

"Sour cream raisin pie," Marian answered shortly, "for the branding bee."

"Branding bee?"

Marian gave a quick look of disgust she might have

bestowed on any city greenhorn and went on running the edge of the crimping tool around the rim of the pie she held in her hand. "Neighbors all get together and help each other," she said succinctly, as if it pained her to explain anything so obvious.

"Is there anything I can do?"

She fully expected Marian's refusal, but to her surprise the woman said, "That bread dough needs punching down."

"I think I can do that." She washed her hands at the sink and did as she was instructed.

"You had a phone call last night."

She looked up at the older woman, her eyes wide with surprise. "I did?"

"Your sister-in-law. She said she'd call back and not to worry, that everything was all right."

"Did she say when she would call again?"

"This evening." Marian didn't stop trimming off the spiral of pie dough around the pan. "You can start peeling those potatoes if you want to," the woman said diffidently.

She picked up the potato peeler on the counter. Surprisingly enough, they began to talk. Catriona found herself telling Marian about Robbie, and she listened while Marian told about her son's child who had had a problem with his hip and had gone in for surgery.

"He's fine now and I'm sure your nephew will be, too," Marian said matter-of-factly. Her eyes flickered over the heaping mound of peeled potatoes. " 'Pears you do know how to work."

She said easily, "I kept house for my father and my brother, too, till he got married, so I do know how to cook."

"Good thing. 'Pears to me some women just use this new liberation thing to get out of doing their share of the work."

"Most liberated women do their share—and then some," Catriona ventured.

Marian snorted softly.

"Well, maybe we can agree to disagree on that," she said lightly.

"I can't think what the world is coming to! Women cowboys!"

Catriona hid a smile and said cautiously, "The world is changing . . ."

"I hope I'm dead and gone before it changes any more. Putting a woman on the back of a horse and asking her to sleep out on the range like a man!" Marian made a sound in her throat that Catriona was beginning to recognize as a sign of her greatest derision. "That's asking for trouble."

Catriona had to admit she had mixed emotions about it herself, but only when the man and woman involved were Logan and herself. "There are lots of women that work as range hands," she said, remembering what Logan had told her.

"Here, let me show you how to make that bread dough into cloverleaf rolls," Marian said, effectively closing off any further rebuttal Catriona might make to her arguments.

Working with Marian helped her control her scattered thoughts. She punched down the bread dough again, rolled it into ping-pong ball shapes, and placed three of the balls into baking cups so that the dough would run together and make the cloverleaf rolls. She made coffee and poured the hot liquid into several thermos bottles and helped Marian pack beer and soft drinks into large tin tubs filled with ice. The tubs would go into the back of Logan's pickup and be taken to the branding site. The crew had moved closer to the ranch now and were in the east corral, Marian told her.

She continued to work through the morning. By eleven

o'clock she felt as if she had worked harder than she ever had on the range.

Marian heard the small sigh that escaped her lips. "Sit down and have a cup of coffee," the older woman urged her with a trace of sympathy. "I think everything's pretty well under control. Grace will be along to help us serve the meal."

Catriona gratefully poured herself a cup of steaming liquid and set it down on the table. She had raised her arms and was retying the ribbon in her hair when she heard the booted step on the porch, and before she could lower her arms, Logan stepped into the kitchen.

His brows gathered in a frown. He was hatless, and the path of his eyes over her was almost physical. She lowered her arms hastily, and all her lectures to herself in the privacy of her bath couldn't keep her blood from racing in her veins and the color away from her cheeks.

As if he hadn't held her, hadn't caressed her, hadn't nearly made her his, he said coolly, "I thought I told you to rest."

She bridled, instantly angry that he could be so cool while her emotions roiled around like sea water trapped in a cove. "I wasn't sleepy."

"Those were my instructions."

"Most employers don't attempt to infringe on their employees' off hours," she said crisply, determined to be as cool as he.

Logan stepped farther into the room, and somehow the spacious kitchen seemed to shrink in size. Marian stood at the stove, stirring the potatoes, her mouth drawn together in a line.

"That's my point," Logan countered softly. "You haven't had any time off since you arrived here."

He was arguing with her about her time off and he looked completely drained. He hadn't shaved for days, she thought inconsequentially, and his beard was dark and heavy on his face. His denim clothes carried the distinct odor of horse and cattle, but still her pulses throbbed and her eyes clung to him as if they couldn't be torn away. He returned her gaze, his own eyes guarded. Then, as if he had other things on his mind, he turned to his housekeeper.

"My men need something to drink, Marian."

"It's all right there," she said tartly, gesturing at the tubs that sat next to the nook. "But I don't give a hoot how liberated you tell me I am, I'm not going to carry them out to the pickup for you."

Catriona hid a grin and Logan's mouth quirked. "I wouldn't expect you to carry those heavy things, Marian." His eyes flickered back to Catriona and suddenly they were sharing a smile. He directed his next words to her. "As long as you're not going to follow my orders to rest, you may as well come with me and drive the pickup back to the house."

Her skin prickled. The thought of riding with him in the intimate confines of the vehicle they had almost made love in the night before made her want desperately to refuse, but she couldn't. She couldn't let Marian think she was any more than a ranch hand who had been hired to work. "Yes, of course," she said, matching his own cool tone.

He picked up the heavy tub and Catriona opened the door for him. Outside she managed the latch on the gate as well, and when he had loaded the tub in the back and slid into the seat beside her, he mocked, "You look like a regular country woman, hair all pulled back and opening gates for your man."

"Looks can be deceiving," she replied as he started the engine and turned the pickup around in the yard.

"Can they?" He was silent for a moment as if he were thinking that over. "I don't think so. A sick cow usually looks sick."

"That's not exactly a fair analogy," she said shortly. "We're not talking about sick cows."

"What are we talking about?" He drawled the question softly.

"I thought we were talking about the way I look."

Logan turned the wheel of the pickup and they bounced over the pasture toward the corral. When they neared the branding site, where men and cattle were working on the wet grass, he slowed his speed.

He stopped the pickup and turned to her, his arm draped over the wheel. "I have to admit I was wrong about you, Catriona."

The husky intimate quality of his voice made her heart set off at double time. "You were?"

He nodded. "In any number of ways. I—"

"Hey, Logan. We're gonna die of thirst out here," Seth Davis was calling to them, gesturing with a long arm.

"The drinks are around in the back," Logan said through the open window. "Get somebody to help you." He turned back to her. "Catriona, I—"

A young man walked up to them. "Logan, we got a calf that looks pretty sick. Maybe you better isolate him and try to get him eating before we brand him . . . Hey, is this the new ranch hand?" The speaker had chestnut-colored hair and Grace Blake's lively eyes. He stood at the truck window gazing across Logan at Catriona.

Logan made the introductions. Scott Blake's bright hazel eyes slid over her dark hair and slim body with avid interest. "Gee, the girls Logan hired last year didn't look like you . . ."

"Go help Seth distribute the liquid refreshment. I want to talk with Ms. Morgan—alone," he finished pointedly.

Scott shot him a curious glance. "Okay," he said good-naturedly and grinned. "You don't have to draw me a picture, big brother. I know when I'm being warned off the territory." With a grin at Catriona he pivoted and walked away.

"That wasn't necessary," she told him. "Now your brother is going to think there's something between us."

"Let him," he said shortly. "Catriona—"

"Logan!" a male voice called. "Where's that other branding iron?"

"For God's sake," he said, thrusting his hand through his hair. He gazed at her, frustration and annoyance furrowing his brow. Finally, he said, "Look, I want to talk to you"—his eyes lifted to the crowd in front of them—"but I can't here." He moved to get out and then turned back. "This thing shifts just like your car except that reverse is to the side. Got that?" He demonstrated with a swift thrust of his hand on the gear shift.

She nodded wordlessly.

He opened the door and swung to the ground with ease. "I'll see you this evening, then."

His broad back was all she saw as he walked away from her toward the place where the three branding crews were working. She watched him go, her heart soaring with hope. Then she slid across the seat and after a bit of fumbling shifted the heavy vehicle into gear and turned it around.

I was wrong about you, he had said, *in any number of ways*... The pickup bounced back over the road, and for the first time since she had come to Wyoming, she wanted to laugh with relief.

Back at the house she parked the pickup away from the gate. Minutes later she helped Marian and Grace set up the tables under the cool shade of the pines on the south side of the house. Marian brought out lawn chairs by the dozens, unfolded them, and scattered them around for people to sit in as they ate. Catriona helped her set up a table with a huge washbasin full of water, soap, and several dark, clean towels where the men and women would wash.

In another hour the lawn began to fill up with laughing, sunburned people. She met Bill Dorin and his two daughters, who were skilled at roping calves; Jason Laurence and his wife, who had identical grins and proudly held their baby daughter up for display to Catriona; Wade Ellis and his crew from Ian McClain's ranch; and several others whose names and faces she couldn't remember. She had half expected to see Diana McClain, but the stunning redhead was not part of the group.

"She's home getting ready for the barbecue tomorrow night," Ellis, a tall, rangy cowboy who had herded cattle in Texas, said in answer to someone's question. Then he turned to Catriona, "You'll be coming, won't you, Ms. Morgan?"

Logan appeared at her elbow. "Yes, of course she will." When Catriona opened her mouth to protest, Logan gazed down at her with a gleam of amusement in his blue eyes. "She wants to experience every part of Wyoming living."

Wade Ellis grinned. "Well, a McClain barbecue is not exactly what I'd call typical of life in Wyoming, but it's a pleasant way to end a long, dust-eating day." His grin broadened. "I was talking about their swimming pool. Wait till you see it. I hope you brought your suit."

Catriona avoided the veiled question. "They have a pool?"

Ellis nodded. "They heat it so they can swim early in the spring and late in the fall."

Logan said smoothly, "Better go help yourself to the food, Wade, or it might disappear before you get your share."

The slim cowboy smiled at Logan. "I know Marian wouldn't let that happen." Then his eyes dropped to Catriona and he said quickly, "But I suppose I'd better not take the chance of missing out on that good chow." He strode away toward the table.

"You'd better go get yours, too," Logan said softly. "I'll wait."

She opened her mouth to object, and swallowed her objection when she saw the warning look in his eyes.

Knowing that Logan meant to eat with her made her heart pound with excitement as she walked to the table and picked up a plate. Marian had provided enough food for an army, it seemed, and what she hadn't thought to prepare, other women had. There was ham as well as sliced roast beef, mashed potatoes, corn that had been frozen last summer, cole slaw, tossed green salad, the cloverleaf rolls Catriona had shaped, homemade strawberry jam, and every kind of pie that ever existed—pumpkin, pecan, lemon, banana cream, and the sour cream raisin, which was, Marian had told her, a special favorite of Logan's.

Carefully balancing her full plate in one hand and her glass of lemonade in the other, she walked to an empty chair. Logan had been leaning against the trunk of a cottonwood tree, but now he moved forward with a lithe grace and took a chair close to hers.

She bent down and put her lemonade on the grass, propping it against the metal leg of her chair. The murmur of people talking surrounded her, and through it all she heard the Laurence baby gurgling delightedly to herself in that language that all babies seem to know.

Her thoughts went to Robbie. Why had Sheryl called? She hoped nothing was wrong, but Sheryl had specifically said that there wasn't any problem.

She found that her appetite was greatly diminished with Logan only inches away. He ate silently, deftly, not bothered by having to balance his plate in one hand and his can of beer in the other.

A breeze rustled the tree leaves together, making a

papery sound. There was no view of the mountains here, but still the terrain stretched in front of her, rolling and green and contained by wooden fences. In the corral next to the barn, a horse nickered and pounded around inside the fence. Robbie would love it here, she thought. Had Logan meant it when he had invited Sheryl and her small son for a visit? She hoped he had. Perhaps after Robbie's operation . . . if everything went well . . . A bit of food caught in her throat and she coughed. Logan tossed his plate to the ground and was leaning over her almost instantly. "Is something wrong?"

A quiet descended. Even the baby seemed affected by it and sat in her slanted chair with wide blue eyes the size of saucers looking at Catriona.

Her cheeks flaming, she whispered, "Sit down, Logan. I'm fine."

He eased his long frame back into the chair, but his eyes stayed on her. To her relief the hum of conversation began again and people applied themselves to the task of eating.

With a mocking smile Logan murmured softly, "I thought I was going to have to give you one of those hugs."

"I'm perfectly able to take care of myself," she shot back, also keeping her voice low.

"I might have some question about that," Logan countered.

Her appetite gone, she set her plate down on the grass and picked up her lemonade. The liquid was tart and sweet and cool in her throat. "I've managed for twenty-seven years without your help."

"But when you needed help badly, you contacted me," he said, and she was silent, unable to deny the truth.

"I'll see you in my study tonight at eight o'clock," he said brusquely, and got lazily to his feet.

She went through the motions of helping with the clean-up. The chairs had to be folded and stacked on the porch, the food all carried into the house and refrigerated for the light lunch that would be served that evening. And there were the dishes to do, stacks of them. Marian filled the dishwasher and then began to do the rest of them by hand. The women all gathered around to help, chatting in easy friendliness. Though she added little to the conversation, she didn't feel left out. To Catriona, brought up in a suitcase and moved from one town to another all her life, the easy laughter and friendship was all totally unfamiliar, but wonderfully comforting.

Her feeling of being an accepted part of the group carried her through the afternoon. But when the yard had emptied of cars and trucks, and Marian said good-bye and got into her car, Catriona was left feeling very much alone. But she wasn't alone. Logan was in the study. And he was waiting for her.

She steeled herself to walk down the hall. She opened the door and entered an environment that was totally male. Every wall except the one behind her was lined with shelves of books. The room was dominated by the stone fireplace and the massive walnut desk that stood to one side of it. There was a leather couch and a circular black fur rug in front of the hearth. But Logan was not sitting on the couch. He sat behind the desk, the tilt of his chair making him a shadowy form beyond the pool of light that illuminated the top of the desk. Instead of trying to make out his features, she stared at what looked like an archaic map of the ranch that was framed and spotlighted over the fireplace.

"Come in and sit down." There was a faint touch of impatience in his voice as if she had done something to displease him. She walked around to the couch and teetered just on the edge of its comfortable cushion, her nerves alive with tension. "What did you want to see me about?"

He leaned forward. The light played over his face. It

was cool, bland, without a trace of emotion. "I've decided to change our agreement slightly."

She stiffened and his brows jerked upward. "No," he said roughly, "don't jump to any conclusions until you've heard me out." He picked up a pen on the desk and toyed with it idly. "I would be willing for you to continue as a ranch hand. You've quickly learned to ride and you make an effort to do your share of work."

She flushed slightly, his words giving her a sense of pleasure that was all out of proportion to their matter-of-fact content. Then she realized what he was really saying and her temper flared. "But you aren't going to let me continue."

"The fact remains that you are not experienced," he went on, "and it's possible that one of the men could be endangered because of your inexperience."

She said hotly, "I can take care of myself."

He drawled, "Like you did with the horse?"

"That was an unusual circumstance."

He pushed himself away from the desk and stood up. Two steps took him to the mantel of the fireplace. He leaned an elbow there and stared down at her, the spotlight gleaming off his dark hair. "I can't follow you around making sure that nothing happens. I have a responsibility for the well-being of everyone on this ranch," he said softly, "as well as my responsibility to you."

"You have no responsibility to me," she returned heatedly. "None."

"It's my job to see that you return to Chicago in November in one piece."

"I thought it was the other hands you were worried about." The thought of leaving was disturbing.

He strode to the couch and sat down beside her. "Do you think you could possibly just listen for one minute without interrupting?"

Stung, she closed her mouth.

"I have an inordinate amount of book work and correspondence to do, and during the roundup I always fall behind. It's occurred to me that you could be of more help to me here"—he nodded his head toward the desk—"than you are out on the range."

"But you said yourself I was learning quickly," she protested.

"You're not safe out there," he said harshly, "and your presence distracts the men."

The blood rose in her face again. "Do I have any choice?" she asked, her voice low.

He shook his head. "No. I've already decided that I need you here."

She got to her feet, far too conscious of the fact that Logan had showered and changed and was wearing that special after-shave that she associated only with him and a silky shirt that would be pleasant to touch. "Then this little discussion is really just a charade, isn't it?"

He lunged to his feet and grasped her shoulders. "Damn it, I was trying to do it the right way, trying to explain that I'm asking you to do something different, not because of anything you've done wrong but because I need you in a different capacity . . . trying for once to communicate with you . . ." His eyes traveled over her newly tanned face, the dark hair that had long since lost its ribbon, the T-shirt that fit her feminine curves exactly. "But it's impossible. We only have one channel of communication . . ."

In the dim light his dark face bent toward her and his hands clamped more tightly on her shoulders. *He's going to kiss me,* she thought wildly, *and I want him to, oh, I want him to . . .*

His mouth claimed hers in hungry possession as if he, too, wanted nothing more from this moment in time than to feel her lips under his. His hands slid from her shoulders to her back and waist and lower. He pressed her hips against him, the hard muscles of his thighs telling her he was as aroused as she was.

He raised his head and his lips found her temple. "I thought I'd go crazy waiting for this damn day to be over so I could hold you in my arms again."

The soft, husky demand in his tone, and the knowledge that he had not forgotten their passionate hours during the storm and that he had been as frustrated as she, made all her defenses fall away. "You can't—you can't mean that," she argued softly.

"Can't I?" He bent his head and sought out the sensitive skin of her neck, nibbling with his lips and then touching her lightly with his tongue. "You don't have any idea what I'm feeling right at this moment."

"I have an idea," she murmured with a husky intentness that made him laugh softly in his throat as he pulled her down to the couch with him and cradled her on his lap with her legs over his. "This is where we started last night, I think." He kissed her with a warm passion, his hand seeking and finding the soft roundness of her breast. But suddenly he ended the kiss and lifted his head to look down at her with a gleam of amusement. "I liked what you had on then much better." His hand trailed down the buttonless shirt between her breasts to the bottom edge. "Lift your arms, honey."

She hesitated. This was not nestling in his arms for comfort during the storm nor an accidental encounter. If she did as he asked, she knew the natural progression of events. She had been Logan's lover once before and he had been hers. But cool common sense made her say, "No, Logan, I—"

He stilled her words with a quick hard kiss on her mouth and then trailed his lips to the top of her arm just at the bottom of the soft cotton sleeve. He turned the hem of the sleeve back and kissed the smooth skin underneath. The touch of his lips sent her blood racing in her veins.

Still clinging to a thread of restraint, she whispered, "No, please, Logan . . ."

His hand grasped her wrist. He lifted her arm and placed his mouth on the soft underside. His other hand holding the sleeve of her shirt, he kept his mouth on her arm, moving it slowly to end in the palm of her hand where he touched the tip of his tongue lightly. She was gasping with pleasure when deftly, he pulled the shirt over her head and dropped it to the floor. Pale flesh gleamed against the lacy undergarment. "Logan, please . . ."

He bent toward her and to escape she half turned toward his chest. Her evasive movement only made it easier for him to unclip her bra. He eased the straps away and the undergarment followed her shirt.

His hand on her shoulder, he turned her outward to gaze on her feminine beauty. Although the soft light behind them was not bright, her white breasts were much more visible to him than they had been the night before. She should not have wanted Logan's eyes on her; she should not have wanted to see that glow of desire deep in the cobalt-blue depths. But she did. She did, and she couldn't lie to herself any longer. She wanted Logan with every cell in her body.

"Yes," he said softly as if she had asked him a question. He bent to her and his warm lips on her rosy peak made her flesh tauten and her lower body tingle with desire. His fingers discovered her other breast, traced around the nipple. A moan escaped her throat. There was a soft click, as if in answer . . . and then the telephone shrilled from its place on the desk.

Catriona shook in reaction, but he murmured comfortingly to her and stroked his hands over her shoulders. His mouth so close to hers that his lips brushed her when they moved, he said, "Let it ring. Marian will answer it." The telephone rang again and she moved to escape his kiss, but he clamped his hands on her shoulders. "Don't move. Let it ring." There was a harsh, grating note in his voice this time, and he made no secret of the fact that he had no intention of letting her go. He feathered a light kiss over her mouth and then moved his lips lower, seeking the delicate skin just below her throat and above her breasts.

She whispered miserably, "Marian's gone home." And then in the next second she remembered the housekeeper's words. "Oh, Logan, it might be Sheryl. Please—"

He held her still for a second longer. Then he swore softly, and his hands relaxed and he let her go. She slid off his lap and stooped gracefully to retrieve her clothes. She knew he was staring at her, but when the phone rang again, she clutched her shirt in front of her and gave him an imploring look. He thrust a hand around to the back of his neck in an angry gesture and got off the couch. His lean body was tight with tension when he strode to the phone. She turned her back to him and scrambled into her clothes, her trembling fingers barely able to fasten her bra and pull her shirt over her head. His hello was less than civil, but after he listened to the answering greeting, his voice warmed. Catriona felt an instant thrust of jealousy. Was Diana on the other end of the line?

She was fully dressed and smoothing her hair when he handed her the phone.

"Hi." Sheryl's voice sounded clear and full of bubbling good humor. "I caught you in the house this time. Logan's housekeeper said you were out on the range. What were you doing out there, Cat?"

She fought the urge to laugh hysterically and said, "Working. How are you? And how's Robbie?"

"He's great, just great. Those pictures Logan sent gave him a real high. He can't wait to get in the hospital, get his operation over with, and get out there to see you both."

Her body still vibrated from Logan's caresses. Her mind

didn't seem to be functioning. "Pictures?"

"Yes, of the ranch. Didn't he tell you he was going to send them?"

She pivoted around silently, her eyes seeking him. He was leaning against the mantel, watching her with indifferent eyes. She turned around again, unaccountably angry that he could be so composed after making passionate love to her only a moment ago. "No—no, he didn't mention anything about pictures."

"He must have sent them the day you arrived back in Wyoming, and I suppose he just forgot to mention them to you. Anyway, Robbie was delighted. It's all he's been talking about for hours." She paused and said with a tremble of emotion, "The operation will be in three weeks"—a nervous little laugh followed—"but it's going to seem like three years."

"I know he's going to be all right, Sheryl. He's got to be."

There was another nervous laugh and then Sheryl said warmly, "You know people always say that—that they just know everything's going to be all right. I've never really believed it until you found the money for Robbie. When that happened my whole attitude changed. Suddenly anything was possible—even Robbie's getting well. It's been my dream for so long." She hesitated and then said huskily, "I—I wish you were here to share the excitement with me, Cat. I miss you and Robbie does, too."

She swallowed. "I miss you both, too. Give him a big kiss for me."

She could hear Sheryl gulping back the tears, fighting for control. Quickly she said, "Has Robbie been in for tests?" Distracted, Sheryl regained her emotional control and was able to speak again. She told about some of the events of the last few days, the tests Robbie had stood so well, the cowboy pictures he was collecting from magazines to add to those of Logan's ranch, and an incident at the shop where a woman had come in and bought a large order of plants. Sheryl paused for breath and then said regretfully that she should hang up. Catriona told her good-bye at once, knowing that the call was an added expense that her sister-in-law really couldn't afford.

She replaced the phone and turned to Logan. He seemed to be a statue standing there by the fireplace. "Robbie loved the pictures. It was kind of you to send them."

He didn't move a muscle. His gaze was cool. "Don't put yourself out, Catriona."

Angrily, she retorted, "I wasn't putting myself out."

"It kills you to thank me for anything."

She turned away. "Because I owe you so much."

His voice rasped harshly behind her. "You don't owe me a damn thing."

She reached out and steadied herself with a hand on the corner of the desk. "I owe you Robbie's life—and perhaps Sheryl's, too, who knows? She was almost at the end of her endurance . . ."

The rough quality of his voice didn't lessen. "When I take you in my arms you forget how much you 'owe' me, don't you?" His voice hardened, became icy. "Or do you? Is it your sense of indebtedness that compels you to respond to me?" Her knees trembled under her and she turned to face him, leaning back against the desk in order to give her shaking legs support. Unnerved, driven by a force she couldn't understand or control, the truth spilled from her lips. "Oh, Logan"—her eyes never left his cool, indifferent face—"when I'm in your arms I can't think at all."

The coolness fell away and his eyes glittered with some emotion she couldn't define. "If I thought for a moment I could believe that . . ." His voice dropped to a whisper, but the words rang in her ears.

"I've never lied to you about the way I feel."

Their eyes locked. A hard, almost palpable tension flowed between them. Then, as if he had come to a decision, he folded his arms and leaned back against the mantel; his eyes narrowed and fastened on her. "Suppose," he said softly, "suppose I absolve you of all responsibility for the debt." He paused to let her absorb that and then asked, "Would you agree to stay with me?"

The blood seemed to rush to her head. Could he possibly be saying what he seemed to be saying? "I made an agreement—"

"And I'm breaking it," he murmured.

She shook her head. "You can't. I'd always be in your debt."

"I want you," he seemed almost to be forcing the words from his lips, "and no amount of money in the world is worth losing you."

She stared at him wordlessly, her mind whirling in a kaleidoscope of thoughts. "Do you mean that—"

He interrupted harshly. "You either go back to Chicago—with no recriminations—or you stay . . . and we establish a new relationship based on our mutual need for each other."

Every fierce resolve, every word of warning, every cool reasoning thought churned inside her head, and dissolved under the fierce heat of the thought that if she left, she would never see him again. She knew that. She would never have another chance to lie in his arms, to feel his warm, possessive kisses, to know the ecstasy of his hands on her body.

"I'll—I'll stay, Logan."

His eyes glowed with an incandescent warmth that went to her head like wine. "Are you sure?"

Her gaze didn't leave his face. "I'm sure."

There was an electric silence in the room crackling between them like supercharged air before a storm. For a long moment they stood, caught in the turmoil of their inner emotions. His husky voice broke the silence. "Come here, Catriona."

CHAPTER SEVEN

She shook her head. At his quick, scowling frown she laughed shakily. "I'm not defying you. I'm just not sure that I can walk that far."

One quick, lithe move brought him to her. He scooped her off her feet and into his arms. She clasped his neck and nestled her head against his chest.

When her hands touched his nape, he said huskily, "You weren't joking, were you? Your hands are like ice." The dark warmth was back in his eyes as he swung her around and walked toward the door. "One small breakthrough—an honest admission of feminine weakness."

"Oh, don't talk like a smug, superior male."

He laughed softly and began to climb the stairs. "But I do have a few redeeming qualities, don't I?" She ignored his mocking words and lay like a doll in his arms, her black hair a dark tangle of silk against his shoulder. Yes, he had redeeming qualities. He was warm and real and male and his shirt was silky under her cheek and his legs and thighs worked easily to bear her upward around the curving staircase. She reveled in his male strength.

He paused just outside his bedroom. The door was

open, the light on, and the spread turned down. A circle of light poured over the dark brown silk sheets, giving the room an intimate quality that made her breath catch in her throat and her heart pound. She said nothing, and he strode forward, his soft footfalls on the thick carpeting deepening her sense of utter aloneness with him. She shook her head in an attempt to control her singing nerves and said with a self-conscious laugh, "How did Marian find time to do this along with everything else she did today?"

"She's very organized and fastidious. She likes you, do you know that?"

"She's a marvel. You're lucky to have her."

"Am I?" He laid her gently on the bed and followed her down, sitting next to her and planting his hands on either side of her head. "Would you believe I didn't bring you up here to discuss my housekeeper's sterling attributes?"

She raised her fingers to his lips and gave in to the luxury of exploring the firm upper curve and the lower, fuller one. "What did you want to discuss?"

He caught her fingers and pressed a kiss into her palm. "You know what I want," he told her huskily. "And it isn't a discussion." His soft tone was like a teasing caress. He smiled down into her face, and she answered his smile with a trembling lift of her lips. He gathered her close to him and at the same time expertly divested her of shirt and bra. Cool air touched her skin but before she could move, he had unsnapped her jeans and was sliding them down over her hips, his hands sensual and provocative on her hip bones. Her senses leaped in response to his hands on her body. Then her last remaining undergarment was stripped away, and she lay naked before him. His eyes glittered as he gazed at her. He reached for her, but she made a soft sound of reproach. She wanted the freedom to view his male beauty. Before he could move to caress her, she lifted her hands to unbutton the pearl buttons of his silky brown shirt and expose his tanned flesh with the dark curling hairs to her gaze. When she had finished, he drew away to complete what she had begun, his eyes never leaving her as he took off the rest of his clothes and let them join hers on the floor.

Watching him emerge from his clothes, she could only think how beautiful he was, tan and lean and strong, a magnificent male and utterly without self-consciousness. He bent and lay beside her, propping his head on his arm to look down into her face. Her reaching fingers played over his chest and found the hard male nipples.

Exalting in his groan of pleasure to her touch on his warm flesh, she said, "I love . . . the feel of you under my hands, Logan."

"And I love . . . the feel of you under my mouth, Catriona," he murmured huskily, covering her lips with a warm, possessive kiss, finding her breast with his hand. He went on kissing her, his tongue teasing her lips. Tentatively, she opened her mouth to grant him the access he demanded. He rewarded her acquiescence by giving every corner of her mouth his careful attention until the light, exploring flicks of his tongue made her shudder with delight. He raised his head and traced a finger down the smooth skin between her breasts. Tingling with sensual pleasure, aching with need, she whispered his name. The pounding of her heart told her it was almost terrifying to want someone so desperately and be so thoroughly possessed. She felt as if he had taken the very heart of her into his mouth and hands.

But it was only the beginning. His mouth dropped lower, caressing her burning skin, seeking and finding the feminine peak his hands had teased to tautness only moments ago. His fingers spread over the smooth flatness of her abdomen. He kissed and caressed her, discovering all the secret places he had known before, seeking her femininity with his own brand of expertise until her hips writhed and her body arched toward him in silent pleading. With a soft groan he moved over her and made her his in a wild coming together that was all the more passionate for their remembered lovemaking and the deprivation that had followed. Starved for each other and drowning in the wonder of being together again, their bodies and minds knew a glorious elation that would not be denied. It rose and swelled to burst over them in a shimmer of light and color and emotion and leave them exhausted and satiated in each other's arms.

She lay entangled with him, the languorous aftermath making her limbs heavy, her eyelids drooping. He eased his weight away, but held her to his lean body, the entire length of him touching her. Gradually, the sensation of floating in a sensual haze drained away. She made an attempt to move.

"Where do you think you're going?"

"To my room . . ."

"No." The soft word was a command. "You're staying here with me."

"But, Logan, I can't—"

"You're not going anywhere."

His legs moved to trap hers and his fingers dropped to her stomach. Idly, he traced a circle over the flat smoothness of her. The answering stirring low in her abdomen brought a sound of mingled protest and longing to her lips. His soft laugh told her he knew exactly what effect his lazy stroking had on her. Just his merest touch on her skin and she wanted him again . . . He murmured a love word to her and traced the word on her abdomen with tormenting curves and loops. Fighting her arousal, she steeled herself to lie utterly still. The feather-light fingers drifted upward, finding their way to the rosy peak that had already betrayed her with its tautness, its readiness for his touch, his mouth. He had breached her defenses, aroused her again . . . and he knew it.

"Logan, I—please don't—"

"All right," he murmured blandly. His hands and mouth left her and he rolled away.

Chilled and devastated, she lay utterly stunned, fighting her desire. He had done it purposely, taken her at her word. She could hear his quiet, even breathing only inches away. He was waiting for her to admit that she had lied, coolly forcing her admission that she wanted him, silently demanding complete surrender. He knew he had aroused her, and that her appetite for him was as insatiable as his was for her. He wanted honesty and communication and he was forcing her to admit the truth . . . that he had never coerced her in any way, that she was in his bed of her own free will, a willing and avid partner in their lovemaking.

He lay with his hands clasped behind his head as if he were sunning on the beach, the brown silk sheet thrown casually over his lower body. She fought for a moment longer, telling herself she was strong enough to repel his assault on her senses, her body . . . and her soul. But the lamplight gleamed over his tanned satin skin and, as if her body had a thought pattern of its own, she raised herself on one elbow to look down into his lean, taut face.

He stopped her words with his soft command. "Whatever you're going to say, make it the truth, Cat." His voice was totally devoid of passion, utterly blunt in meaning. A chill feathered over her naked skin.

She leaned over him, pressing her breasts against his chest. Surely he couldn't be as unmoved as he appeared to be. Cool blue eyes returned her gaze without a flicker of disturbed emotion in their depths. His hard indifference shook her resolve badly. Only her love for him gave her the courage to say in a husky thread of sound, "I want you, Logan—want you, need you, lo—"

He moved with the swiftness of a striking panther. His

hand clasped her nape in almost painful possession and he brought her mouth down to meet his in a hard, passionate kiss.

After he had taken her to the heights a second time, and they came down gently together, he lay breathing softly into her hair. Then he reached over to turn out the light and moments later his even breathing told her he was asleep. She moved to leave the bed.

With reflexes like a cat, he roused and caught her wrist. "No. You're staying here."

He pulled her against him and nestled her spine against his chest, turning to fit her head into the hollow of his shoulder. "Comfortable?"

"Yes." *So comfortable I never want to leave.*

"Go to sleep, Cat. I'll see you in the morning."

But when morning came, he was gone, and she gathered her clothes to leave his room. On her way out of the door she caught a glimpse of his robe hanging just inside the bathroom and on a sudden impulse decided to slip it on. It would at least be a covering in case she happened to walk straight into Marian when she stepped out the door. She wrapped the long silk robe around her and tied the tie, but she needn't have bothered. The house echoed with empty quietness when she went into the hall. Minutes later, after she had gone to her room, showered, and changed into clean denims and a plaid shirt, there was still no sound from any of the rooms in the big house.

She descended the stairs and pushed open the familiar swinging door to the kitchen. The room was empty, but a pot of coffee stood heating on the stove. She poured herself a cup of the hot brew and went to the eating nook to sit down on the curved seat. Behind it four windows gave a panoramic view of the mountains. The sun shone on everything, heightening the colors, making the barn a deep red, the grass a rich green, and the sky a cerulean blue. It was high summer and Wyoming was beautiful.

The step at the door brought her head around. Logan stood there in jeans and a denim shirt with the sleeves rolled away from his muscular arms.

For a breathless moment her eyes flew to his, and she knew that if that cool indifference was back this morning, she wouldn't be able to bear it. But the warm gleam that met her gaze was anything but cool. "Did you finally decide to get up?" he drawled lazily.

There was a taut sheen to his skin and a lazy smile on his lips. He went to the stove and poured himself a cup of coffee and turned with it in his hand, the steam rising in front of his shirt. "May I sit with you?"

"Of course—yes." She slid over and made a place for him on the curved bench and he sat down next to her.

"Did you get some sleep after all?" Amusement colored his low tone.

Color rose in her cheeks. "Yes."

He smiled, and for once there was no mockery in the lift of his lips. "I thought so. You were sleeping like a child when I got up this morning." He raised his cup to his mouth and the rolled cuff of his shirt brushed her arm.

She fought her response to his words and the reality of him next to her. "Where's Marian?"

"Taking the day off. She always does after the branding bee."

The drift of his after-shave came to her. She turned her head to gaze at the mountains. "The view from your window is gorgeous."

"Yes, isn't it?" The soft words of agreement didn't seem to be directed toward the view.

Tenaciously, she clung to the prosaic conversation topic. "I've never heard of the Bighorn Mountains before. Are they as high as the Tetons?"

"No." The soft word came from very close to her ear. "Catriona."

She had to turn then, and he was so close she brushed his cheek with her hair. "Yes?"

"Kiss me good morning."

"I . . ." He waited for her to go on with her token protest, his eyes on her mouth, his lips lifted in a slight smile, as if he remembered every passionate sound she had moaned into his ear the night before. Her words died on her lips. She gripped his shoulders and leaned forward to press her mouth to his. He didn't touch her, didn't put his arms around her. He was making her the aggressor, and the passive resistance of his mouth made her more determined than ever to arouse him. She pressed closer and touched her tongue lightly to his lips. His shuddering response sent a flash of satisfaction through her. She was destroying his cool control just as he destroyed hers. He brought his hands up and grasped her shoulders to thrust her away.

"I have work to do today," he said huskily, "and unless you want me to forget it and spend the day in bed with you—"

"You told me to kiss you good morning," she murmured. "I was only following your instructions."

"So you were." He moved then, sliding to the edge of the bench and unfolding his lean body to stand beside her. "I'll have to learn to be more careful about what I tell you to do."

Her body felt cool and deprived without the warmth of his. She fought it by looking up at him with a tilted head and a slight smile. "Yes, you will, won't you?"

He gazed back at her, a warm, possessive look in his eyes. "Are you ready to start your new job?"

"As ready as I'll ever be, I guess."

He turned away and she rose to follow him down the hall and into his den. She averted her eyes from the deep leather couch and followed him to the desk. "Sit down," he said, rolling out the swivel chair for her. He pulled a bulging book from the lower desk drawer and laid it open in front of her.

For the next half hour he leaned over her shoulder and showed her what he expected her to do. She had had no idea there was so much bookkeeping to be done on a ranch. In addition to the records on feed bought and used, Logan kept a careful count on the number of cows in the herd, as well as calves that were born, purchased, and sold. There was a payroll to make out and all the inevitable records that went with that—social security, medical insurance forms, and claims, as well as deductions on the living quarters that were maintained for those employees who lived on the ranch.

"You could use a computer," she said.

"I had planned to get one, but—"

He closed his mouth suddenly, and she knew at once that his loan to her had been the money he would have used to purchase the expensive piece of equipment. Disturbed to think that he had rearranged his life to give her the money for Robbie, she felt more compelled than ever to make herself useful and struggled to concentrate on his instructions. For today her task was to make out the payroll checks.

He handed her the long black checkbook and showed her the ledger where the names and amounts were recorded.

He straightened as if to leave. "Do you have any questions?"

She shook her head.

"I'll leave you to it, then."

He took a step around the desk and walked the length of the room. He had his hand on the doorknob when her voice stopped him. "You trust me with your blank checkbook?"

He turned slowly. "Is there any reason why I shouldn't?"

Driven on by an urge she scarcely understood, she said lightly, "I could make out a check to myself and disappear, couldn't I?"

His lips lifted in a smile. "If you were going to do that," he drawled, "you'd hardly sit there telling me about it, would you?"

She rubbed her perspiring palms together under the desk. "Logan, if you trust me with this"—she gestured toward the book—"surely you can trust me to tell you the truth about other things."

He leaned back against the door and folded his arms. "Such as?"

She gripped the edge of the desk with her hands, feeling the beveled wood edge. "Such as believing that"—she swallowed and forced herself to go on—"when I said I loved you two years ago I meant it."

He didn't move a muscle from his lazy stance. "Did you?"

"You must have known I did," she said huskily.

"But when I asked you to come with me, you refused," he countered with cool logic. A muscle moved on the side of his cheek. "And you're only here now because another member of your family is in need."

"Yes, that's true, but—"

He straightened away from the door. "What do you expect to gain by rehashing the past?"

"Perhaps . . ." She faltered for a moment under his unrelenting gaze and then lifted her chin. "A future."

His eyes glittered with a hard light. "We tried that once and it didn't work."

"Then there can't be a present for us, either."

In two lithe steps he came to her and lifted her out of the chair and into his arms, his hands hard on her waist. "But there is," he said huskily, "and you're enjoying it as much as I am." His mouth traced a path over her cheek. "Let the past go and don't try to second guess what's ahead of us. The important thing is that you're here and that we've been honest enough to admit that we need each other . . ."

"No—"

"Yes," he murmured against her skin, and then turned her face up and took her mouth, branding her once more with his possession.

He released her slowly. "I can see"—his voice was a husky caress—"that if I don't leave this house soon, I won't get out of it at all today." He strode out of the room and she sat back down at the desk, her body shaking, her mind in a turmoil.

She forced herself to pick up the gold pen that was Logan's and began to write out the checks that he would sign later. Oh, why was he such a maddening, infuriating man? He had made it quite clear that she was nothing more than a temporary amusement in his life. How could she go on for another half year, working for him, loving him, and knowing at the end of her alloted time he would send her back to Chicago without a second thought?

The pen scratched over the next check. He was willing to trust her with everything but his heart. Was there a way to breach his mistrust? Or had she ruined any chance of a permanent relationship with him two years ago?

There was no way to go back and replay the past, nor would she if she could. She would react no differently today than she had then.

But what of her dilemma now? She was caught securely in a trap of her own making. She wanted, needed Logan's love more than ever. If she stayed—if she stayed—was there a chance she could convince him that she cared for him, and at the same time take Diana's place in his heart? Could the passion that she and Logan shared become something deeper?

She shook her head wearily, knowing that after all her thinking, she hadn't made a clear-cut decision. She would simply have to live each day as it came, and savor every moment of her time with Logan.

The morning wore on and she completed her task. Logan returned to the house and in the kitchen they worked together to prepare a light lunch. When the sandwiches were made, Logan sat down next to her in the curved nook just as he had that morning. His closeness robbed her of her appetite.

After a moment of silence he asked, "What's the matter?" His eyes moved over her face and rested on her mouth. "After all the work you did this morning you should be hungry."

"I must miss being out in the open air," she said lightly.

"Maybe this will stimulate your appetite," he mocked softly and bent his head to brush his lips lightly over hers.

It was her heart that was stimulated, and its racing beat seemed to mingle with the sound of the back door opening and closing in the porch.

Logan lifted his head just as Grace Blake walked into the kitchen. There was a heartbeat of silence as her eyes played over them. Whether the woman noticed that they were needlessly sitting on the same side of the table close to each other and that Catriona's sandwich was nearly untouched, and her face was rosy with embarrassment, she couldn't tell.

Then, easily, as if she knew exactly what had happened just before she entered the room and approved of it, Grace Blake smiled and said briskly, "Good afternoon. What a pleasant surprise to see you in the house at this hour, Logan. I thought you would be out on the range and Catriona would be rattling around here all by herself."

Logan leaned back on the bench and favored his stepmother with an amused, tolerant look. "Is that why you came over?"

Grace Blake shook her head. "Well, no. I left a casserole dish here yesterday that I need to fix my potatoes in for the barbecue party tonight. And I wanted to make sure Catriona had a swimsuit."

"Thoughtful of you," Logan murmured.

"Well, she can't go swimming at the McClains' if she doesn't. At least"—the woman chuckled—"she shouldn't or Ian McClain will have that heart attack he's always threatening to have and never does."

Logan smiled. "We wouldn't want that to happen, would we?"

Grace Blake tilted her head as if she were considering it, her eyes bright with laughter. "I'm not sure. It would serve the old curmudgeon right after the way he's had young Doctor Masterson trotting out to see him week after week."

"Tom doesn't seem to mind."

His stepmother shot Logan a shrewd look. "No, he doesn't, does he? He's quite smitten with Diana, I hear." The woman gazed at Logan. "If you're not careful, you'll lose her to him."

There was a short, loaded pause. "Diana was never mine to lose," Logan drawled.

"Wasn't she? Well, thank goodness for that," Grace said brightly. "Now that I know you aren't in danger of dying from a broken heart, I'll ask to borrow Catriona for the rest of the day if I may. I wanted to go shopping and I hate to drive to Sheridan alone." Grace hesitated and then asked quickly, "Or did you need her for something this afternoon?"

"No," came the soft reply. "I don't need her for anything this afternoon. She is going to the barbecue with me tonight, though."

Did the older woman hear the soft emphasis on "need" and "this afternoon"? Catriona fervently hoped that she hadn't.

"I'll have her back in plenty of time to get ready for tonight," she assured him. Then she asked Catriona, "Is that all right with you? Would you mind riding in to town with me?"

Catriona felt very much as if Grace Blake was a small, feminine steamroller who simply flattened any opposition to her schemes with her friendly smile. Catriona couldn't refuse without seeming churlish. "No, of course not."

Hazel eyes looked directly into hers. "Do you have a suit?"

Catriona shook her head. "No. But—"

"Good. Then we can look for one."

"No, really—I can't. I—"

"Grace, I think Catriona is reluctant to admit that her funds are limited right now. Why don't you go with her while she makes her choice and charge it to my account? I can take it out of her paycheck."

"I never gave money a thought. Thank you, Logan." Then she said to Catriona, "Well, shall we go?"

No, we shouldn't, she thought fiercely. *And I won't buy anything with Logan's money.* Stalling, she asked, "Shouldn't I change?"

Grace laughed, a low, pleasant sound. "Not for Sheridan folks, honey."

With a smooth movement Logan straightened and rose to his feet. He stood looking down at Catriona, a dark gleam of amusement in his eyes. "I'll look forward to seeing you tonight then." And he said to Grace, "Make sure Catriona doesn't change her mind. If she needs a suit, she should have one." He neatly slammed the door on her plan to refuse to spend Logan's money when they arrived in town. "And behave yourself, Grace. Hold your speed down. You know you've already gotten your speeding ticket for this year."

"Shush! You'll scare Catriona into staying home."

Logan raised a dark eyebrow. "Maybe she should. You be careful with her in the car."

With a wicked twinkle in her eye, Grace asked, "Are you worried about her?"

Logan didn't rise to the bait. He drawled, "I'm responsible for her. I'd like to keep her in one piece while she's in Wyoming, if at all possible."

"I don't really drive all that fast," Grace told her when they were in the small car and had turned out of the lane onto the macadam-surfaced road. Her swift acceleration belied every word. "It's just that this car rides and drives so smoothly I do sometimes go faster than I realize. But isn't it nice of Logan to be so concerned about you?"

Catriona was not a nervous rider, but she did notice the fence posts seemed to be whizzing by at a fast rate. "I'm sure he's concerned about all the people who work for him."

"Are you? Well, I suppose you're right." She didn't sound convinced. "Logan doesn't take his responsibilities lightly. I think sometimes he drives himself twice as hard just to prove he doesn't have his mother's blood in his veins." She paused. "He continually fights his heritage and he has no reason to. He's a fine man."

Catriona struggled for something to say that would deter her from such introspective dissection of Logan. "It's unusual that you have such a good relationship."

Grace nodded. "I suppose in a way I'm lucky. Logan disliked his mother intensely, and he was more than ready to accept me after I married Jonas. Yet I do wish Logan would forgive Leah. She isn't a bad person. She's just a bit flighty, frivolous, I guess you'd say. She simply wasn't cut out to be a rancher's wife, that's all."

Startled, Catriona said, "You said isn't. I had the impression that Logan's mother was dead."

Grace laughed. "Good heavens, no. She's living in Las

Vegas with her third husband. But I can understand why you thought that. Logan never speaks of her. He's blocked her out of his mind, or at least he thinks he has." She sighed. "But sometimes I think everything he does is aimed at proving to himself that he isn't Leah's child." The older woman flicked a sideways glance at Catriona. "I'm sure you're wondering what she did that was so terrible. Nothing, really, except try to live a life she wasn't suited for. She was from New York City originally, and I don't know anything about her parents, but I think she was a young, spoiled girl, very used to having her own way. She was genuinely in love with Logan's father, but he was just getting started in the cattle business and Leah couldn't stand the isolation while Jonas was out on the range. Jonas was working all the hours God sends to insure the financial security he felt Leah deserved.

"She stuck it out until Logan was three, and then one day she just got in the car and drove away. Logan's father was bitter, naturally, and he made sure that Logan learned the meaning of responsibility. When Jonas died, Logan naturally expected Diana to marry and settle down with him. But she, like his mother, told him she could never be a rancher's wife. She left him and went to Los Angeles . . . married another man within a matter of months. The marriage didn't last. When she came back, everyone was sure Logan would take up with her again. I think Diana's more than willing now. But I'm not sure Logan will give her another chance." She paused and sighed. "He hasn't been lucky with his women."

"Except for you," Catriona said warmly.

"And you." The two words were blunt.

"I'm not—I don't—"

Grace made an impatient sound. "I'm not blind, you know." Then with a light laugh she said, "Or are you going to tell me that kiss I almost walked in on this noon was nothing but a friendly one between a female ranch hand and her boss?"

Catriona said nothing. She couldn't deny what Grace Blake had seen for herself. She stared out at the rolling landscape that moved by in front of her.

"I'm not so old I can't recognize a kiss being shared by two lovers," the woman said softly. "Can you honestly tell me that you're not in love with him?" When Catriona didn't answer, Grace went on, "Your eyes give you away, you know. They're very expressive. They seem to turn a shade darker when you look at him." She sighed. "I suppose you think I'm nothing but a nosey old body who should mind her own business. And I suppose I should. Logan gave me to understand that he wouldn't stand for my meddling. He knows me too well." Another soft laugh escaped her throat. "But I want Logan to be happy. And he hasn't been—not for a very long time." Her hands tightened on the wheel. "I owe him so much. When Jonas died, I started having problems with Scott. He was rebelling at school, and at home, he gave me trouble over the slightest thing. He missed his father desperately. He was sixteen—at the worst possible age to be without a father, it seemed to me. I asked him to do less and less around the ranch, thinking he needed lighter responsibilities, forgetting that work can be the best cure for grief. Scott got in with the wrong crowd and began to drink. Logan stood it as long as he could, till finally he insisted on moving over to the house where he lives now and giving Scott the responsibility of running the ranch where we live. I was terrified by the idea. But Logan knew that was exactly what the boy needed. Scott balked at first, but he is his father's son, after all. He accepted the challenge eventually and enjoyed it. He's a real credit to me, and to Logan."

"I'm sure he is. But—"

"Well, we're almost there. I hope you can find something at Alice's that you like." She slammed on the brakes to avoid an oil tanker that had turned out of a side street in front of her. Sheridan had the appearance of a boom town. The streets were lined with pickups, semitrailer trucks, and oil tankers.

"I wish they'd find their shale oil, or gas and whatever, and just leave us alone. Between the government wanting more parks, and the energy crunch, everybody's looking for land in Wyoming." She accelerated and then suddenly pulled into a parking place in front of a row of buildings that seemed to comprise the business district of the town.

Alice's Shop, the letters above the big glass display window proclaimed, and from the cracked condition of the sign Catriona decided the store had been in operation for a number of years. Inside dresses hung in cabinets along the walls on the side, and the newer turnstile type of displays were few in number and filled with blouses rather than pants and jeans.

"No one knows who Alice is," Grace told her cheerfully as a plump, white-haired woman came out of the back. "Mary's been the owner for as long as I can remember."

"The swimsuits are on this rack," Mary told Grace after she had explained what was wanted. "What is she—about an eight?"

Grace shot her a warning look, and reluctantly, Catriona nodded.

"Shouldn't have any trouble finding her size. I just got a new fandangled thing in from New York City. Bikini with a matching dress. Want to see it?"

"No," Catriona said.

"Yes," Grace contradicted her.

"It's ice blue," Mary said, ignoring Catriona's negative answer and turning away to sort through garments, pushing them aside one by one. "Should go good with your color hair and eyes."

Mary found what she was looking for and brought it out to hang on an outside hook for better viewing. "You're new here, aren't you?"

"She's working for my son this summer," Grace interceded, stepping forward to examine Mary's selection. The dress was a shimmering ice blue with spaghetti straps and a brief bodice. The skirt swung away from the defined waist with the graceful swing of a dancer's costume. Underneath were the two tiny pieces of matching cloth that were the bikini.

"The suit is strapless—not sure how it stays up when you swim, or *if* it stays up," Mary said with a short laugh. "It's designed so you can wear the bikini underneath the dress. When you want to go for a swim, you just take the dress off and"—she swung a hand down her ample hip—"there you are. Ready to jump in the pool. Want to try it on?"

Catriona shook her head, but Grace said, "Yes, she does. Go ahead, dear. I'll wait out here."

If she didn't want to look like a fool, she had no choice but to go into the little cubicle with the garments. She stripped off her shirt and jeans and put the tiny silken bra on—a scrap of material that just covered her breasts. The briefs slid easily over her hips. When she had put on the dress and adjusted the straps, she had to admit the skirt felt silky and feminine as it swirled around her legs.

When she walked out of the dressing room, Mary exploded with a satisfied, "I knew you'd look good in that color," and Grace Blake said simply, "We'll take it. Charge it to Logan, Mary."

Something flashed in the shopowner's eyes, but she just smiled a broad smile and said, "Sure. I know his credit's good. Take it off, honey, and I'll wrap it up for you. Gonna wear it to the barbecue tonight?"

"Yes, she is," Grace said to Catriona's retreating figure.

She was disturbed when she came out and the dress and suit were wrapped and handed to her. Anxious to leave Mary's sharply questioning eyes behind her, she opened the door too quickly and was nearly run down by a tall cowboy striding past just at that moment.

She staggered and nearly fell, and he stopped at once and caught her elbow. "'Scuse me, ma'am," he said politely, touching his hat.

"That's quite all right," she murmured. "I—"

Behind her Grace Blake exclaimed, "Dr. Masterson! Hello, how are you?"

Her rescuer released her elbow. "Just fine, Grace. How are you doing?"

In his boots, jeans, and Stetson hat he didn't look like a doctor. She stood politely while Grace spoke with the tall young man. He was very slim, with long thin hands that he had thrust into the pocket of his jeans as he stood talking to Grace Blake.

"May I introduce you to Catriona? This is Dr. Tom Masterson—Catriona Morgan."

Grace explained that Catriona was working on the Double B ranch for the summer and Tom Masterson didn't flicker an eyelash. "Nice to have you in our community, Catriona." He put his hand to his hat. "Grace, if you'll excuse me, I've got a call to make."

"Oh, of course we understand, Doctor. I'm sorry if we've held you up."

Tom Masterson grinned and Catriona thought he was really quite attractive. "No problem. I'm just glad I didn't have to administer treatment to my victim."

After he had smiled at Catriona and said good-bye, Grace stood watching him walk away with thoughtful eyes. "He is a most pleasant young man. And we're fortunate to have him here. He had an offer to practice in San Francisco, but he refused. He wanted to live in cowboy country."

"I can understand that."

"Can you?" Grace paused by the car and studied her for a moment. Then she said crisply, "Well, let's not stand out here on the street. Get in."

When Grace had started the engine, Catriona said, "Didn't you have some shopping you wanted to do?"

The older woman shrugged her shoulders. "I've changed my mind. I really didn't have anything definite in mind, and I suppose I should be getting back. Scott will probably be wanting something for his men to drink. They're making hay this afternoon and they can work up a thirst."

She wheeled expertly around the corner and made Catriona breathless as she cut in and out of the trucks with an expertise that Catriona would normally have expected of a race-car driver.

On the road back to the ranch Grace asked sympathetic but probing questions about Catriona's family. When Catriona had told her almost everything, including the seriousness of Robbie's condition, Grace made a sympathetic sound in her throat. "How terrible for you and your sister-in-law. But Robbie's going to be operated on soon, you say."

"Yes. We're all hoping everything will be all right."

"I'm sure it will be, dear. You will let us know the minute you hear anything, won't you?"

"Yes, of course."

Grace was uncharacteristically silent the rest of the way home, and Catriona looked out the window on her side of the car, but she saw nothing of the outside world. Her thoughts were turned inward. Grace drove at a high rate of speed despite Logan's admonition, and they were soon at the ranch.

When Catriona climbed out of the car, Grace thrust the package at her. "Don't forget that. I'll want to see you in it tonight—and so will everyone else." An acutely self-satisfied smile on lips, she said good-bye, and the instant Catriona stepped away from the car she circled around the yard and shot down the lane. Catriona stared after the disappearing car in rueful consternation, and it was only then that she remembered Grace had not picked up a dish in the kitchen, or even looked for one.

She walked into the empty house and went through the hallway, knowing quite well she had been actively cultivated by Grace Blake. Logan's stepmother had come purposely to take her to Sheridan—away from Logan—to talk to her. And why? She didn't have to search far into her mind for the answer to that. *Because she knows I love him.*

She climbed the stairs, thinking how different things would have been if Grace were a greedy, grasping woman who wanted Logan's affection for herself. But Grace wasn't like that. No, Grace loved Logan—truly loved him. She wanted Logan's happiness.

But where did that lie? She went into her bedroom and saw her neatly made bed, the bed she had not slept in last night. She had slept in Logan's arms . . . because it was something they both wanted.

She walked into the bathroom, laid out a towel, and turned on the water. Logan wanted her sexually, that was true, but that simply wasn't enough. Lust, desire, whatever name you wanted to give it, wasn't enough for two people to build a lifetime together. There had to be trust and understanding—and love—as well as physical attraction. Was her love alone enough for both of them?

She had a much clearer understanding of what his life was like now. Before, living in the city, she hadn't really known. She hadn't known about the hard work and the occasional loneliness. She supposed she must have appeared to be a typical city girl to Logan, and worse, she thought suddenly, one who was dependent on limelight and applause.

She stripped out of her clothes and climbed into the deep tub. She lay in a mindless haze, letting the sensuous pleasure of the scented water occupy her mind. But she could not keep her thoughts at bay for long. *Logan's happiness.* If she, Catriona, truly loved him, that's what she wanted, too. But did he need Diana to be happy? Or was Grace Blake right in her belief that Logan would not risk resuming his relationship with Diana? Or was Grace simply not seeing that Logan was giving Diana time to adjust to life in the country again before he asked her to commit herself to him? Was Diana the woman he had always loved, the woman he needed to make his life complete?

Just the thought of it made her stomach squeeze in pain. But she had to admit that Logan and Diana had seemed much more than friends. Diana had called him "darling." And Catriona had the distinct feeling that she wasn't a woman to call everyone darling indiscriminately.

And suppose Logan had taken Catriona to his bed to have one last fling before he settled down with Diana. A warmth filled her cheeks that had nothing to do with the temperature of the water. She wouldn't be used that way —she wouldn't!

She rinsed away the bubbles and climbed out of the tub. She had only two alternatives really, she thought, as she rubbed herself with the fluffy towel. She could either stay here and try to win Logan's love, or she could leave Logan and go back to Chicago. *Leave Logan.* That was a cold, lonely, intolerable thought. In the bedroom she saw his robe lying where she had thrown it over the chair that morning. On an impulse she unwound the towel she had wrapped herself in and put on the masculine wrap. The scent of him clung to the silk. She tied the belt around her waist and stood for a moment, feeling an incredible sense of weariness overwhelm her. The hot water had made her relaxed and sleepy. She would decide what to do after the barbecue . . . after she had seen Logan with Diana again.

Perhaps then she could tell if Logan still loved his former fiancée. But right now she couldn't think anymore. She went to her bed, crawled beneath the covers, and laid her head on the softly scented pillowcase. Long dark lashes flickered down, and she slept.

CHAPTER EIGHT

Something feathered over her eyes. She moved restlessly, coming back from the depths of a dream. The light, teasing touch on her face didn't stop. She came awake and opened her eyes to see that the room was almost dark, and that Logan was sitting on the bed beside her, wearing nothing but a towel wrapped around his lean hips, bending over her, brushing his mouth on her forehead.

She fought the temptation to close her eyes and pretend she was still asleep so he would go on kissing her—and lost. She shut her eyes quickly and tried to maintain an even breathing pattern, but his husky laugh told her she hadn't fooled him for a second.

"I know you're awake, honey. A cat can't play possum," he murmured, touching her earlobe with his tongue.

Her ear tantalized by his flickering tongue, her nostrils registering the warm, clean smell of him, she lifted her arms and clasped him around the waist. "Umm, you smell good."

"I thought that was my line."

She let her fingers explore the hard muscles that lay

under the smooth skin. "We don't have 'lines,' Logan. We never have had lines, have we?"

"If you mean you're totally unpredictable, I agree. I never know what you're going to do from one moment to the next. For instance"—he traced a finger down the path between her breasts, the sides of their round fullness exposed by the gaping collar of the robe—"I never would have expected to find you all curled up in your bed, sleeping like a child—and wearing my robe. That's a very sexy thing to do, honey."

She fought the electric shock that tingled along her nerves at his suggestive words and retaliated crisply, "Well, coming into a woman's bedroom wearing nothing but a towel isn't the most exemplary behavior, either."

He chuckled and nibbled lightly at her nose. "You think not?"

"I know not."

"What else could I do?" he mocked softly. "My robe is already occupied. Unless"—he hesitated, and a wicked gleam shone in his eyes—"you want to give it back to me—now."

An answering smile of amusement tugged at her lips. "And if I don't?"

"I might be forced to reclaim my property in my own way."

"I wouldn't if I were you," she returned spiritedly. "Cats may not play possum very well, but they do know how to defend themselves."

"I've learned that at the expense of my shin," he groaned in mock pain. He smiled down at her. "But they also purr when they're stroked." His hand brushed aside the brown silk and found the roundness of her breast. Her flesh seemed to burn at the sure touch of his fingers.

Unbidden, the thought that he would be with Diana tonight came to her mind. "Logan, don't, please."

"Did I say you were unpredictable?" There was an

amused exasperation in his voice. "My God, you're the most perverse, contrary, obstinate . . ." He bent his head and took her nipple into his mouth, teasing it to a taut peak and then raising his head to look into her flushed face. "Beautiful, responsive bit of femininity I've ever held in my arms."

"Logan, please—"

He stilled her words with his mouth on her own, gentling her lips till she gave him the access he wanted. With his tongue reverently probing her mouth, her senses clamored for him, but her mind said coldly, *He calls you beautiful . . . but if he loves Diana, you're a fool . . .*

When he lifted his head, she struggled for control. "Logan, isn't it late? Shouldn't we be getting ready?"

He shook his head, his smile warm. "That's not what we should be doing and you know it."

"Logan, please . . ."

He drew back from her slightly. "You really do want a reprieve? Because that's all it will be . . ."

"I need some time to get ready."

He gazed at her for a long moment, desire still glittering in his eyes. Then he rose reluctantly, his fingers going to the towel at his waist. "All right. Is an hour long enough?"

"Yes—yes, an hour will be plenty of time."

His eyes played over her and then the dark lashes shuttered them, hiding his thoughts from her. "I'll meet you downstairs then."

When he turned and walked to the door, she almost called him back. He was so damnably attractive, and she loved him deeply. Why should she refuse him what might possibly be their last time together? But he had stepped into the hall and closed the door behind him, and there was nothing left to do now but put on the bikini and its matching dress and pray his eyes wouldn't be filled with love when he looked at Diana tonight.

* * *

When she walked down the stairs, her hair long and full around her bare shoulders, the silk skirt teasing her slim, tanned legs, she saw Logan's tall figure standing in the living room. His back was to her and he was looking out at the ranch, his profile dark and brooding. Then he turned, and as if it took him a moment to collect his thoughts from wherever they had been, he seemed not to see her for a moment. When he did take in her appearance, an inexplicable flash of pain crossed his lean features. He said nothing to her, however, and when she reached the bottom step and halted there uncertainly, he gestured toward her with the glass she now saw he had in his hand. "May I get you something to drink before we go?"

The sharp sting of disappointment touched her. She had hoped—prayed—that he would say something about her appearance, anything. But he hadn't. He must already be anticipating his evening with Diana.

She shook her head. She was going to need every particle of her mental acuity to get through this evening. She couldn't muddle her brain with alcohol, at least not yet. That might come later. "No, thank you," she said stiffly. She stood behind a chair, clinging to the velvet back for support. When he made an impatient move toward a table with his glass, she said quickly, "Don't rush. Take your time. I can wait."

She wanted to tear her eyes away from him but she couldn't. He wore a suede suit in a velvety brown color and a cream silk shirt open at the throat, and she could see the dark mat of hair there when he tipped his head back to swallow the last of his drink. His open jacket moved easily over his lean frame as he set the glass down with a sharp click. "Let's go."

In the car she discovered that Logan drove only slightly slower than his stepmother.

"Are you going to huddle over in the corner all the way to McClains', or are you going to tell me what I've done to earn your displeasure in the short span of sixty minutes?"

"I don't know what you're talking about . . ."

The road was virtually deserted, but Logan braked sharply and pulled over to the side. He disengaged the motor and let it idle while he turned to stare at her. She couldn't see him clearly in the dark car, but she faced his silhouette bravely.

"Don't think you can pawn me off with vague, polite phrases," he rasped, "not anymore. What did I do?"

"Nothing . . ."

His hand moved like lightning and he grasped her elbow in a painful grip. "The truth, damn you."

Shaken, she blurted, "It's nothing. I just thought you might say you liked the way I look, that's all. I know it's silly, but—"

"My God! Don't you know that seeing you like this only drives it home that I can't keep you"—he buried his mouth against her hair—"but I can't let you go."

Then as if to prove to himself that he could, he thrust her away, leaving her shaken and confused. Nervously, she brushed a lock of dark hair away from her forehead, where his breath had warmed the skin only a second ago. He put his hands on the wheel and clenched it so tightly that she thought it would break. For a heart-pounding aeon, the silence in the car vibrated like a high, thin wire. Whatever his thoughts were . . . they were torturing him.

She opened her mouth to speak to him . . . say his name, beg him to explain, when he suddenly twisted to look over his shoulder, put the car in gear, and accelerated down the road. She felt cold and frightened. Always, just when she thought she was beginning to understand Logan, he did something totally inexplicable like this. She felt foolish, unreasonable tears gathering behind her eyes.

She forced them away and gazed out into the dark. He turned into a lane, pulled up in front of a brightly lit house surrounded by several well-kept buildings, and stopped the car. His hand was impersonal on her elbow as he helped her out. They went up the brick walk toward the low sprawling house together silently. At the door the coach lamps showed clearly the twist of his mouth.

Logan clamped his lips together as if he wanted to say something and thought better of it. He reached forward and pressed the bell, and after a second or two it was opened by a middle-aged manservant in a white coat. He greeted Logan with old-fashioned deference and nodded to Catriona. "Go right on through. Everyone is by the pool."

Logan escorted her through the house, which was furnished lavishly with heavy English-style country oak and decorated in pastel blues and greens. They stepped through a sliding glass door onto a patio of brick. A crowd of perhaps twenty people stood around the broad concrete apron of a kidney-shaped pool. Some of the women were in swimsuits, some wore brightly colored skirts and blouses. She recognized the Laurences and a few others she had met the day before.

"Logan, my boy." A masculine voice boomed out from somewhere under a string of hanging patio lanterns. "Thought you weren't coming. Come—what can I get you to drink?"

Logan guided her across the edge of the concrete over to a portable bar set up away from the pool on a grassy area. From behind the bar with its gleaming arrangement of bottles, a man strode briskly forward to extend his hand to Logan. "Good to see you, good to see you. What can I get to whet your appetite a bit?"

"Some of your excellent bourbon should do the trick," Logan said easily.

"Fine, fine." The elderly man rubbed his hands together and returned to his station behind the bar. Catriona made a small movement to release her elbow from Logan's hold, but he only gripped it tighter.

"Ian, you haven't met Catriona, have you?"

Keen pale-blue eyes looked up from under graying eyebrows. "Don't believe I have."

Logan made the introduction easily, and Ian McClain's eyes moved over her with an acuteness that made her move uncomfortably next to Logan's side. "She's working on your ranch, you say?"

Logan hadn't said so, but he didn't correct the older man. "Yes."

Ian McClain handed Logan his glass and chuckled. "Your 'hands' are getting better and better looking every year."

Logan shook his head. "Do you think so?" There was a tolerant smile on Logan's lips.

Ian McClain made a sound in his throat. "Where are you from, young lady?"

She told him.

"City gal, eh? My daughter tried that city life. She soon discovered she was more country than she thought she was." He nodded behind them and both Logan and Catriona turned. "Beautiful, isn't she?" Diana McClain, in a black maillot suit cut high on the hips and fitting her like a second skin, stood on the diving board above the pool. Her lovely figure seemed to be even more graceful in the soft light as she lifted and kicked off the board to dive cleanly into the aquamarine water below.

Ian McClain's voice took on a conspiratorial tone. "When are you going to break down and ask that girl to marry you, boy? That young doctor's been around her like a fly to a honey pot."

Logan gazed at the old man and his hold on Catriona's arm tightened. "You haven't offered Catriona anything to drink, Ian. Would you like something to drink now, Cat?"

She shook her head. "No, really, nothing for me."

Ian McClain would not be put off. "This ranch is waiting for you when I retire, boy, you and Diana."

"I've told you for five years to put your land in the hands of a manager," Logan returned blandly. "You and I wouldn't last a day together."

Ian McClain drew back as if Logan had struck him. "I've always considered you the son I've never had . . ."

"I'm sorry, Ian." He raised the glass to his lips and drank. When he lowered it, he said softly, "Some things just don't happen the way we want them to happen."

Ian McClain was still staring at Logan in shocked silence when Logan returned his glass to the bar and said to Catriona, "Let's go swimming before supper. We can change our clothes in the cabana under the trees." Red, yellow, and green stripes decorated the building Logan pointed out to her. There were two doors, one blue, the other a bright orange.

Her body burned all over. She had not wanted to be a silent witness to Logan's confrontation with their host, but his firm grip had kept her by his side.

She was thankful when Logan loosened his hold and moved to walk toward the changing cabana. But McClain stepped forward and stopped him. All his hearty effusiveness had disappeared, and something of the mask of an old man along with it. He looked like a tough businessman who had been denied a prize he had counted on winning. "I'll want to talk to you later."

"Anytime, Ian," Logan said easily.

"You think it over, boy. This is a productive ranch . . ."

Logan glanced down at Catriona's flushed face. "Don't bait me, Ian. Take your hook out of the water."

Ian McClain grasped Logan by the sleeve. "Don't be so damn offhand clever with me, boy. My daughter loves you—"

"You're mistaken, Ian." Logan looked down pointedly at his arm.

The gnarled fingers tightened and then dropped away. Sparks of anger shot out of the pale eyes. "I can make you sorry for this—"

"But you won't. Leave it, Ian. Now, if you'll excuse us, I'd like to take Catriona swimming"—a challenging, lazy smile flickered across his face—"or are you rescinding your hospitality for the evening?"

The old man stood there silently, his conflicting emotions mirrored in his face. Then the trace of a rueful smile lifted his lips. "I could never best your father in a stand-off fight, and you're no easier. You're a hard man, Logan Blake . . . but you'll always be welcome on McClain land."

Logan's slow smile seemed to please the other man. McClain's answering smile was thin, but he hit Logan on the upper arm with a semblance of joviality. "Go on—enjoy yourself. We'll talk later."

Logan nodded. He turned away with the smile still lingering on his lips, but he had already put Ian McClain out of his mind, for his eyes were on Catriona's face. "Let's change for our swim."

Her mind in a turmoil of confusion, she walked with him into the shadow of the trees toward the cabana. Because of the cabana's distance from the pool, and the sheltering grove of trees around it, they were essentially alone. Sounds of laughter and splashing water seemed to echo from a distance. Outside he turned her toward him with a hand on her arm. A breeze lifted a lock of her dark hair and feathered it across her cheek. She lifted her hand to brush it back, but Logan's hand was there before her, his fingertips evocative against her cheek. He leaned forward and brushed her temple with a kiss. Then with a mocking smile he murmured, "The orange door is yours, honey. Go on and change. I'll see you in a few minutes."

Her senses reeling from the light touch of his fingers and

lips, disjointed thoughts chasing around in her head, she stepped into the brightly lit cabana. Was it her imagination, or had there been a sudden quiet behind them at the pool area? Somehow, this evening had become far more fraught with undercurrents of emotion than she had anticipated. She tried to concentrate on the task of undressing. Because of the design of her dress, stripping to the bikini was a simple matter that took only seconds. There were towels folded neatly on a wicker stand and a full-length mirror at the opposite end of the room. Self-consciously, she adjusted her suit and glanced in the mirror. The reflection of that slim, nearly naked feminine figure made her avert her eyes and walk to the wicker stand to pick up one of the oversized beach towels. She stepped out to find Logan already there, leaning against a tree waiting for her. He straightened lazily, making her instantly aware of his long, lean body. He wore a pair of black silk briefs that left his masculinity in little doubt. His muscular chest was tanned and covered with dark hairs and the bare masculine legs were curved with muscle.

In the shadow of the trees his eyes reflected a gleam of light from the pool lamps that told her he was seeing what she had seen when she looked in that full-length mirror—the brief ice-blue suit made her skin look like ivory satin, and her long, slim legs were displayed to the best advantage. His eyes traveled over her and came back to linger at the high breasts, their fullness accentuated by the blue strip of cloth gathered in the center.

She was accustomed to being on display, of course, but not in quite such an abbreviated costume, and her skin warmed at the undisguised desire in his eyes. "I'm crazy to let other men see you like this," he muttered in her ear as he took her arm and guided her in the direction of the pool.

Boldly, she shot back, "What about you?"

"Logan!" Diana McClain's unmistakable husky tone

floated out over the water. "Come on. These men need you."

A shout of derision went up, and a green and red striped beach ball bounced from hand to hand above a pool full of reaching arms. Logan pulled Catriona forward. "It's a game of keep away, honey. Men against the women."

He splashed into the water and turned to lift her down. The water was cool and silky and welcome to her heated flesh, which had warmed instantly in response to Logan's hands on her bare waist.

They were in the shallow end of the pool. Logan grabbed her hand and tugged her into waist-deep water, and then suddenly someone tossed the ball to him and he rose out of the water and caught it. Diana splashed after him and lunged toward him in an attempt to get the ball. Logan waited until the last possible moment and Diana was nearly at his side before he handed the ball neatly to a man behind him. Catriona took a swipe at it as it went by and missed. By this time Catriona had discovered it was a wild game of free-for-all with no holds barred. Possession of the ball was everything, and anyone who held the ball unwarily, or overly long, soon lost it.

Two of the men she recognized as part of the McClain's branding crew seemed particularly to enjoy catching Diana with the ball in her hands. She tossed it off to one of the other women in the pool, who promptly flipped it to Catriona. Logan came up from under the water and snatched it from Catriona's hands, to the groans of the other women in the pool. Diana was after Logan again. She threw herself on him and suddenly Catriona heard him mutter a stifled curse. Diana resurfaced above the water, but Logan still held the beach ball in his hand. He pretended to toss it to the right and when Diana lunged at him from that direction, he shifted his course and tossed it easily to the young ranch hand who stood on his left. The game continued, with Diana pouncing on Logan whenever he had the ball, while he apparently enjoyed tormenting her by holding the ball just out of her reach and then passing it off behind her back.

There was the clanging sound of a dinner bell. Ian McClain's voice boomed out that it was time to eat. The game disintegrated, and everyone climbed out of the pool. Catriona hung back, unwilling to jostle for position at the ladder. Conscious of Logan behind her, she clasped the slippery coolness of the pool ladder and pulled herself out of the water.

The air was a crisp, shocking cool after the warm silkiness of the water, but no one seemed to think of changing. Towels were picked up and flung over shoulders, and in twos and threes people followed Diana and trailed across the lawn to the table standing just outside the patio doors that was laden with food. Two of the ranch hands jostled each other for a place in line, and Diana said laughingly, "Hey, guys, take it easy. There's enough for everybody."

When it was Catriona's turn to fill her plate, she helped herself to a little bit of everything—the savory-smelling barbecued beef, the hot potato salad, and the fresh fruit cut up and nestling inside a fresh pineapple. Logan watched her fill her plate with an amused smile. When he filled his own and they walked over to seat themselves in lawn chairs, he murmured, "Hungry?"

She smiled. "It looks like it, doesn't it?"

"I'm hungry too," he murmured softly, "but not for food." His hand dropped to the smooth curve of her hip, which was bare just below her towel, but the movement made him wince slightly.

"Logan, what is it?"

"Nothing," he said, his voice suddenly clipped. He applied himself to the task of eating, and after a moment of puzzled thought she did the same.

When they finished their meal, there was ice cream made the old-fashioned way and dipped out of the wooden churn. Smooth and creamy with a pure vanilla flavor, it had a deliciously wicked richness.

"You look like a cat enjoying its cream," Logan murmured as they stood on the lawn eating out of soup-bowl-sized dishes.

"It's very good," she murmured.

The manservant who had met them at the door appeared with a large trolley and began to clear away the dishes of food. The volume level of the music increased and Diana strolled over to Logan. "Dance with me, darling."

He stood gazing at her for a moment and then said easily, "Is it ladies' choice?"

"Yes," Diana said, her teeth flashing in a bright smile. "And I've chosen you."

"I think I'll wait," came the soft reply. "I might convince Catriona to ask me."

Every bit of color seemed to leave Diana McClain's cheeks. The long fingers with their perfectly groomed bronze nails clutched at Logan's arm. But Diana's voice was cool. "Logan, please. Don't embarrass me this way."

Catriona said quickly, "Go ahead. I think I'll go and change. I feel a little chilled."

"Do you?" The question was soft. Logan's eyes gleamed over Catriona for a moment until Diana's clasp on his arm drew him away.

The cabana was in the opposite direction from the patio and she was glad. She couldn't bear to watch Logan turn and fold Diana into a dancing embrace.

A portable heater had been turned on inside the cabana, and the air was warm and steamy. Her suit had dried. In slow motion she plucked her dress from the hanger and slid it over her head, adjusting the straps over her shoulders. She wanted to stay where she was, to hide away until the music ended and the dance was over, and Logan was no longer holding Diana . . .

Dressed, she slipped her feet into her sandals and was standing in front of the mirror, slowly and thoroughly combing her hair, when she heard the voices. At first they were faint. Then they became more and more distinct, and she knew that Logan and Diana had sought the shelter of the trees and were standing immediately outside the cabana door.

"It's your pride that's keeping us apart, Logan," she heard Diana's low voice say.

He interrupted with a quick, clipped, "Don't, Diana. There's no pride involved, only a simple lack of interest."

His cool words made Catriona shudder inside. She didn't want to be an unwilling eavesdropper. She wanted desperately to get away. Her pulses were throbbing. But Diana, like her father, was not easily cowed. "You don't mean that, Logan, you can't. We've known each other all our lives, and loved each other for as long. You can't just toss that aside . . ."

"You did."

A sound like a gasp followed his clipped, cool words.

"Logan, please. I was young and foolish then. I didn't realize that I could want to live in Wyoming for the rest of my life . . ."

"You've only been here six months. Are you telling me you're ready to settle down on a Wyoming ranch?"

"Yes—oh, yes, Logan—I—"

He stopped her joyous agreement with a crisp, "What about Tom Masterson?"

The comb slipped from Catriona's fingers to the hard Formica top of the dressing table. Logan was in love with Diana and jealous of the young doctor who had been seeing her.

There was a startled silence. Then someone shouted Diana's name.

Logan said, "I think we'd better talk about this some other time. You're being paged."

"But, darling—"

"Go on, be a good hostess. I've got to get changed."

Diana made what sounded like a soft sound of distress and then there was quiet. Catriona waited silently, her hands shaking, her legs unsteady. Somehow, she had to find the courage to walk out of the cabana and pretend she had heard nothing.

She straightened her shoulders and opened the door. There was no one close by, and she forced her legs to carry her around the pool and back to the patio area where most of the crowd sat or stood. The slim man whom Catriona had run into that day in Sheridan was standing beside Diana, holding her hand, talking to her and one or two others gathered around him.

"Sorry I'm late. Mrs. Dugan finally had her baby. A boy. Did I miss all the fun and games? Yes, I'll take that drink—thanks, Ian."

With Diana watching, he lifted the glass of clear liquid with its slice of lime to his mouth and drank deeply. When he lowered the glass, he looked at Diana and smiled. "Is it legal for you to walk around looking like that?" With his free arm he pulled her close. Diana resisted, then lifted her hands to his neck and returned his kiss, while one of the cowboys cheered. Tom released Diana and grinned.

"Hello, Logan. How are you?"

Startled, Catriona turned to find Logan, fully dressed, his face expressionless, standing quietly behind her. The passionate kiss Diana had bestowed on Tom Masterson was for his benefit, Catriona thought with despair. But if Logan felt any emotion, it was hidden behind his cool face. "Good. And you, Tom?"

Masterson kept Diana close with an arm at her waist. "Right at the moment, I couldn't be better."

Diana threw a look past Catriona to Logan that was pure triumph and said, "Tom, how sweet. Have you had anything to eat?"

"As a matter of fact, I thought maybe Callen could fix me a plate in the kitchen."

With another quick look in Logan's direction, Diana linked her arm in Tom Masterson's. "Well, I certainly can't let you eat alone. Let's go see if there's anything left for a hardworking doctor to eat."

Masterson smiled at Diana. "That's too good an offer to refuse. Lead the way, honey."

Talking together, laughing, they walked away. Catriona could not conceal a shiver of tension.

"Are you cold?" Logan asked, his voice coming from just over her shoulder.

"Yes, a little."

"Would you like to leave?" The question was utterly bland and polite.

"Yes," she said again.

Logan escorted her to the bar where Ian McClain stood. He told his host that they had enjoyed the evening, but that he and Catriona were going to make it an early night. Ian's eyes narrowed, registering the easy way that Logan linked their names, but he merely nodded and said he hoped he would see Logan again soon.

Logan helped her into the silver-gray car and went around to the driver's side. When he slid under the wheel, a soft groan escaped his lips. Catriona, disturbed, said, "What is it? What's the matter?"

"It's nothing," he muttered, and started the car.

If she had thought he was taciturn on the way there, he had been garrulous then compared to the ride home. The headlights cut through the darkness and the only sound was the hum of the engine. When they reached the house, he cut the motor and grasped her wrist. "I want to talk to you."

"It's Diana you should be talking to, isn't it?" she replied crisply.

His answer was a soft curse. He got out of the car and

was around to her side before she could open her door. He did it for her and said roughly, "Get out."

There was nothing to do but obey him. She extended shaking legs to the ground, and when she had lifted herself out of the car, he slammed the door and grasped her elbow. He led her across the porch and through the door. When he didn't pause at the living room, but continued on down the hall toward his study, she struggled to free herself.

"Stop it, you little fool," he ordered her sharply, and carrying her resisting body into the den with him, he closed the door behind her. When he had thrust her down onto the couch, he stood looking at her with a cold, brooding expression.

"I want to apologize for Diana," he said harshly.

"It isn't necessary," she said, half rising to her feet. His hard hand on her shoulder pushed her back down on the couch.

"It is." His eyes played over her face. "Ian's spoiled her. He's always given her anything she ever wanted. She can't believe that there's something in this world she can't have."

With chilling clarity she realized that Logan was trying to defend the beautiful red-haired girl because he still loved her. "You needn't be so concerned about my feelings, Logan."

"I am concerned about you. I want to marry you."

He stood over her and looked down at her coolly, as if he had not just delivered a bombshell into her lap. Not a trace of love or desire showed anywhere in his hard mouth, his cool eyes. She stared up at him, wanting his love desperately, wanting to believe that he was asking her to marry him because he loved her. But he met her gaze with that cold, implacable stare, and as if he had shouted it, she knew the real reason he was asking her to marry him. He loved Diana, but he was too proud to admit it and give their love a second chance. He was using her, Catriona, just as Diana had accused him of doing.

"I'm—I'm sorry, Logan. It—it just isn't possible."

His face was utterly expressionless. "Why not?"

"My God!" she exploded. "You can't be serious. You love another woman!"

His eyes were shadowed under the dark curve of his lashes. "What makes you think that?"

"Because it's obvious," she cried, forcing his hand away from her shoulder and jumping to her feet. "Oh, God, just let me alone . . ." She turned and ran to the door, but he was behind her, grabbing her wrist and turning her toward him with a quick twist of his hand.

He pushed her back against the door. "How is it so damn obvious that I'm in love with another woman when it's equally obvious to everyone that I can't stay away from you?"

She heard the faint slip of suede against silk as he moved toward her. *If he kisses me,* she thought despairingly, *if he kisses me, I'll end up saying yes, and marrying a man who loves another woman with all his heart . . .*

His mouth came down on hers, hard and hungry and demanding. A wild surge of excitement made her return his kiss with a demand as insistent as his own. His lips softened at once entreatingly and her own parted to give him her sweetness. His body was a hard weight, holding her against the door. She felt his arousal and the answering ache from deep within her.

He lifted his mouth from hers and brushed his lips over her cheek to her ear. "I want you. I need you. Hold me . . ." His voice was husky with desire and the sound of it made the pulse beat heavily in her throat. He feathered a kiss along her jaw and down to the spot that throbbed so visibly. His caressing hands pushed aside the narrow straps, and her dress fell away, revealing the tiny bikini top. He eased her away from the door and made short work of the clip. "Do you have any idea how that strip of cloth has been tantalizing me all evening . . ." His mouth sought the rosy peak that quivered, waiting for him.

"Oh, Logan . . ." She eased off his jacket and let it fall to the floor. Her hands went to the buttons of his shirt. Eagerly, her hands sought the hard male flesh beneath. She needed, too, needed to hold him closer. Her hands went round to his back and she slid her palms over his skin. He flinched—and at that moment, she felt a deep welt.

"Logan, what—"

"Diana's handiwork while we were in the pool," he muttered. "Forget it."

She shook her head. "No. Let me see." Before he could stop her, she had eased his shirt away and walked around him. A scratch, long and deep and angry-looking, had been scored across his back. The sight of it sickened her. She understood now why he had winced several times when something had come in contact with his back.

"She's marked you well," Catriona said dryly. "You'd better let me put something on it for you."

"The only thing I want on my body is you," he said huskily, and moved to kiss her.

She shook her head. "Do you have some disinfectant in your medicine cabinet?"

His smile was wry. "You're not exactly"—his eyes played over her naked breasts—"dressed to be playing Florence Nightingale."

"Never mind me," she retorted and pulled her dress up to cover herself. "If you don't treat that scratch, you could get a severe infection. Well? Where is the disinfectant?"

"Upstairs"—his eyes gleamed—"in my bedroom."

"Logan," she warned.

"In the bathroom—scout's honor."

"You'd never qualify for that august organization," she said crisply.

He stooped to pick up his shirt and jacket, his voice strangely cool. "As a matter of fact, I made eagle scout."

"I'm sorry," she said. "I didn't mean—"

"It doesn't matter. It isn't the first snap judgment you've made about me."

That low, throbbing tone seemed to echo in her ears as she climbed the stairs ahead of him. She found the light switch in the bedroom and turned it on, flooding the room with light. Unerringly, but terribly aware of Logan's soft steps behind her, she stepped into the room. She turned and went to the bathroom, opened the medicine cabinet, and found the bottle she was looking for on the second shelf.

When she returned to the bedroom, her eyes flew to Logan's lean form stretched on the bed on his stomach. She hesitated for a moment and then walked to the side of the bed, sat down, and uncapped the medicine.

"This might sting," she warned.

His head was turned toward her and a smile lifted the corner of his mouth. "So professional. Are you sure you didn't miss your calling?"

She pulled the dabber from the bottle and stroked the brown liquid on the cut on the shoulder closest to her. He didn't flinch, but she knew he had to be hurting. "Perhaps I did. I really never gave much thought to what I wanted to do . . . I just did what the rest of the family did." She stroked the cut with medicine and he endured it stoically.

Logan was silent for a moment, his body still. Then just as she had almost finished, he said softly, "Why did you come with me, Cat?"

Her heart seemed to stop beating, then to rush forward again. "You know why."

"Tell me again," he ordered softly.

"Because of Robbie," she answered, her hands shaking slightly as she capped the bottle. "No, don't roll over. You'll get medicine all over the spread."

He disobeyed her and turned, capturing her hands the instant she had returned the bottle to the nightstand and before she could rise from the bed. "You were willing to sacrifice part of your life for Robbie. Why won't you do the same for me?"

"The situation is entirely different," she replied, her voice low. "I can't marry you knowing you're in love with another woman."

"Would you believe me if I told you I wasn't?"

She shook her head. "I don't think you know it yourself, but you are. You've loved her all her life, but now you're afraid to trust her again."

He traced a finger down her bare arm and then captured her hand in his. He raised her palm to his mouth and pressed a kiss against the sensitive skin of her hand. "Then, be my sweet sacrifice, Catriona. Help me forget her," he whispered huskily and lifted his arms to pull her down to him.

"Logan, no—"

"Yes, Cat, yes." His mouth covered hers and she was lost, pulled into the vortex of his sensual demand and her own aching need for his love.

CHAPTER NINE

She woke to the sound of birdsong, and a bed empty of Logan. His warm scent clung to the pillow beside her. He had been warm and tender and passionate and demanding. But he had not said he loved her. He had asked her to be his wife. She had told him no with her mouth, but her body had said yes to him over and over again. Dear God, why was love such a torment? Why couldn't it come easily? Why did it have to fester inside like a thorn buried deep in your soul?

Logan's robe lay on the chair next to the bed. Had he placed it there purposely for her, knowing she would need it? Her dress lay in a silky blue heap on the floor. The delicious smell of hot coffee wafted to her nose, and she could hear the sounds in the kitchen that told her Marian was at work.

She should get up. She stretched, threw back the covers, and plucked Logan's robe off the chair. She slipped it on and decided that this morning she would shower in Logan's bathroom.

She stepped inside, trying to push the decision she knew she must make to the back of her mind until she was more fully awake and released from the sensual remembrance of Logan's lovemaking. She slipped out of his robe and stepped into the shower, letting the warm water wash over her, wishing it could wash away all her doubts and fears. Logan had kissed and caressed every inch of her body last night. Was it possible for a man to make love to a woman like that when he loved another? She didn't know. She only knew that she loved him. Could she risk grasping the bit of heaven he had offered her, knowing that her heaven would become a living hell the moment Logan finally realized he did love Diana? Could she risk the devastation of knowing he would, in the end, hate her for preventing him from marrying the woman he really loved? Would she be able to stand being thrust out of his life when he tired of her? Suppose—suppose she had a child. Would Logan insist on keeping the child for him and Diana to raise together? The thought brought a clenching knot of pain to her stomach. She couldn't bear that. But she couldn't bear leaving Logan either, not now, not after knowing the joy of being in his arms again . . . Oh, God, he had her on the rack—and he knew it. He had pleasured her in every way possible last night, knowing full well she could never deny her physical need of him. Her physical need and her emotional need were welded together like iron. But Logan's emotions were a mystery. Could he ever learn to love her as well as desire her?

She stepped out of the shower and dried herself off briskly. She loved Logan. She would take the supreme risk and accept his proposal of marriage. She would become his wife and hope that someday he would return a small portion of her love . . . In Logan's robe she wandered over to the window to look out at the mountains that would become her home. She heard the sound of a car and pulled the curtain aside to get a better view. A sleek gray Mercedes slid to a stop in the yard and Diana McClain stepped out from under the wheel. She wore her red hair loose and full and the sun blazed off those shimmering long strands. Catriona gripped the curtain tighter and then loosened her hold to step back when she saw Logan come out of the barn and walk toward Diana.

Caught, frozen, she watched. Diana's face was animated and joyous. She spoke to Logan with great earnestness, obviously pleading with him, her hand on his arm. Logan listened for a moment, and then he looked down at her and smiled, and there was such genuine amusement and love in that smile that Catriona caught her breath. Then, as if to confirm her own words, Logan reached out and took Diana in his arms and kissed her. The kiss was not long, and when it was over, Logan helped Diana in the car and walked around to get in on the other side.

She knew at once that Diana had, at last, succeeding in convincing Logan of her love for him and her willingness to stay in Wyoming. She clung to the curtain, her hands wet with perspiration, her body cold with shock, trying to tell herself that she had not seen the destruction of her dreams in the short span of a minute. Her mind told her coolly that she had.

The cold knot grew inside her. Logan had kissed Diana and gone with her—to tell her father the happy news, perhaps? She didn't know. *She didn't know.*

She stood in the middle of the room, picturing Logan lying beside her, his hands tracing erotic patterns on her skin . . . Logan riding next to her, risking his life to pull her off a runaway horse . . . Diana walking down the aisle to Logan . . .

She ran across the hall to her room, pulled her suitcase out of the closet, and spread it on the bed. Clothes were wrenched from hangers and thrown into the case. The things that Logan had bought for her were laid aside in a random tangle. She would not take anything with her that he had bought.

How scrupulously honest you are, her mind mocked her.

Honest—except about the one thing that is more important to you than anything else in the world.

Am I supposed wait around until he tells me to go?

Yes! Yes! Don't run away before you learn the truth.

But he loves Diana.

If you love him, have the courage to stay and wish him well.

She stood silent, wearing his robe, her arms clutching a bright-blue dress she had brought with her and never worn. It was not a new garment; she had worn it to the airport that disastrous time she had come to see Logan. She went to the mirror and held it up against her. With her tan, the dress gave her an electric, come-hither, silky look. It was a city dress with all the cut and fashion of high design.

She stood for a moment, hesitating. Well, if she was going to go down, she would go down with all flags flying. Didn't Queen Guinevere dress in her most beautiful gown to be led to the stake before Lancelot saved her?

She stripped off Logan's robe, got into her underthings, and pulled the dress over her shoulders. The top was elegantly simple with a bateau neckline and full puffed sleeves, and the skirt fit her slim waist with a gathered fullness that flared out at her knees.

She finished with a careful application of makeup and walked down the stairs and into the kitchen.

Marian's eyes flickered over her unsuitable attire and then returned to the pie dough she was rolling out.

Catriona took a breath. "If Logan wants me, would you tell him I'm taking a walk?"

The housekeeper looked up. "I'll tell him. You aren't going far, are you?"

Catriona managed a smile. "I'll follow the road, Marian."

"Well, see to it that you do. It's easy to get lost if you don't know the lay of the land."

"Yes, I suppose it is," Catriona agreed, thinking it was just as easy to get lost in life if you didn't know the lay of the land, too. And she didn't seem to have the knack of learning.

Outside she followed the path through the gate and walked toward the lane. Within a few minutes she was out on the road, walking on the side of the macadam. Her sandals were comfortable and the road was smooth. The sun beat down on her head and only a wisp of a breeze feathered a strand of hair over her cheek.

She walked on, up and over the rise of a hill. A view beckoned beside her. She crossed the shallow grassy ditch and went to stand and rest her arms on the rail fence. Blue sky stretched before her, almost cloudless. Below the sky the earth was a lush green, the grass dotted with red where cattle stood grazing.

An ache filled her inside. She had learned to love this land, to love its openness and its freedom. She could have been happy here, she knew that. She had always been adaptable. She had to be. She had lived out of a suitcase most of her life. If only she could have had the chance to prove to Logan that she would be able to live on a ranch . . .

A bird warbled a long, intriguing melody. She turned to look for it and saw a horse and a rider loping easily up the road toward her. The man wore no hat. The sun beat down on his glossy black hair, making it the exact same shade as the horse he rode.

The rider slowed his horse as he approached her and she gripped the wood railing for support. It was Logan.

He rode to the side and dismounted, looping the reins over the horse's head to ground rein him.

She watched, trying desperately to keep her face cool.

In two long strides he crossed the grass verge and came to her. "What are you doing?"

In his boots and jeans and a faded denim shirt open at

the throat, he was as much a part of the land as the grass and the sky. Her throat ached just to look at him. He belonged here—he and Diana.

She leaned back against the rail to support her shaking legs and watched his eyes move over her slowly, taking in her sleek city look from the slight dip of her neckline to her bare feet in the low sandals. "I was just looking."

"What did you see?" He took a step closer.

"I see a land. A land that"—she took a quick breath and then lifted her chin and went on—"a land that belongs to a man I—I'll always love."

Quickly, before he could react, she turned her back and clenched the rail. She couldn't go on looking at him and say what she had to say. Free of the hypnotic sight of him, a breathless torrent of words poured out. "Logan, I know what you're going to say. And I—I want you to know that I understand and I'm not surprised. I knew all along that you loved Diana. I want you to know I—I'm not—I—I won't—it's all right." She faltered and then forced herself to go on. "I wish you both the best of everything."

The bird warbled again, as if in admiration. But Logan made no sound. The silence stretched until her nerves were taut with the strain. She turned.

He was still there, a dark, forbidding look on his face. "What are you talking about?"

"I saw you this morning out the window kissing her—Diana. I started to pack," she went on, recklessly, "but I knew I couldn't go without—without telling you that I understand."

"You do?" She had hoped he might smile but he didn't. Those two brief words were spoken with no expression at all. "I'm glad you do *because I sure as hell don't!* You say you love me. Yet you believe I'd ask you to marry me when I still loved Diana and then toss you aside the minute she crooked her little finger! Is that it? Do I have it right? Is that the kind of man you think I am?" His icy gaze rooted her to the ground.

She cried, "You only asked me to marry you because you felt sorry for me . . ."

"No." His denial was flat and carried the ring of truth. "I've felt a lot of things for you, but pity was never one of them." His eyes narrowed. "I've asked myself many times why you're so convinced I love Diana, and I keep coming up with the same answer. You need to believe I love her . . . because that relieves you of feeling guilty about making love with me when you don't love me. You can't accept a truth that should be obvious to an idiot. Even my stepmother knows I've loved you since the first moment I saw you."

She gasped. "I—I can't believe that. You've never said . . ."

He took a heavy, shuddering breath. "What difference would my saying it make? You couldn't make a commitment to me two years ago and you can't now." Before she could protest, he reached out, grasped the wood railing, and turned away from her to gaze out over the countryside. "I thought letting you come here would help me get you out of my system. I thought if I put you on the back of a horse and took you out on the range, I'd see how unsuited you were to live here. I thought if I reminded myself daily that you didn't fit in, I'd stop wanting you." He lifted his hands toward her and then let them fall to his sides. "Nothing worked out the way I thought it would. You were wonderful on the range, good-natured and uncomplaining and quick to learn. My men fell in love with you. And so did I, all over again. I wanted you more than ever. I still do." She made a sound and he closed his eyes and shook his head. "It's no use. I want you for the rest of my life, not just when you happen to need me, or when I fit into your schedule." He took a step away from her. "And you don't want that. You never have. So I suggest you finish packing. Unless you want to stay for the wedding. Diana came over to tell me that she and Tom are getting married next week. I was kissing the bride."

Abruptly, he pivoted away from her, picked up the reins of his horse, and swung up into the saddle.

"Logan—" He didn't turn back. Her voice was drowned in the sound of hoofbeats.

Alone, she tried to calm the churning in her stomach. Her immediate problem was to get back to the ranch. She stood for a moment and then began to run across the grass.

"Where's Logan?" she said to Marian when she burst into the kitchen, her sides aching from running.

"Probably out in the barn. He said he'd be in for dinner and that he'd take you to the airport afterward. Leaving, are you?"

"No. Yes. I don't know." She shook her head as if denying her confusion. "Will you tell Logan I want to see him upstairs when he comes in?"

"I'll tell him," Marian said, "but I'm no message person. Seems to me people could do their own talking to each other around here."

"We will," she called through the swinging door as she climbed the stairs. To herself, she muttered, "At least, I hope we will."

Her heart beating heavily, she walked into her room. The suitcase still lay on her bed, the clothes in a muddle around it. Resolutely, she began to fold things, packing them in slow motion, taking her time. The task took her almost a half hour. She was just fastening the clasp when she heard Logan's step on the stairs.

He stepped into the room. She thought he must be able to hear her heart beat, it was pounding so loudly against her chest. She forced her lips to lift in a smile.

His eyes swept over the closed suitcases and then up to her face. "You're going then."

"Yes," she answered, watching him. "That's what you wanted, isn't it?"

There was a short, electric pause. He turned away. "I'll go get the car . . ."

She stepped forward and caught his arm. He looked down at her hand, a flash of anger in his eyes. She released him at once. "I—you won't need the car."

"I can't fly you to Chicago, Cat. I can't take the time . . ."

"No need," she said simply. She picked up her makeup case. "Carry the larger one, would you, Logan?"

Her eyes gleamed, but her knees were shaking as she marched past him, straight across the hall into his bedroom. Boldly, she lifted the makeup case and set it down on his bed. She turned to find Logan, standing in the doorway, her other case in his hand. If she hadn't been so frightened, she would have laughed at the expression on his face.

"What do you think you're doing?"

She smiled her practiced smile again and sat down on the bed. "I believe it's called moving in."

A twitch of a muscle on the side of his jaw betrayed him. "How long will you stay?"

She didn't move. "Forever." Her voice trembled over the husky vow.

"If I thought I could believe that . . ."

She met his gaze steadily. "If you'll let me . . . I'll gladly spend the rest of my life proving it to you." She sat waiting, scarcely daring to breathe.

With an agonizing slowness he came into the room, set her suitcase down, and moved toward her. In a harsh rasp she hardly recognized he said, "You'd better mean that. I couldn't stand losing you again . . ."

"You won't, Logan."

He sat down beside her on the bed and pulled her across his thighs so that she was sitting in his lap, her head resting in the hollow of his shoulder. "I said I wanted you to go, but when I walked into that room and saw you with your cases packed and that smile on your face—my God, do you know what you did to me?"

"No." She laughed up into his face, joy sparkling through her. "What did that do to you, darling?"

"You scheming female . . ." He took her mouth, warmly, possessively. She responded, pressing her body against him, caressing his nape with her fingers.

He groaned and murmured, "How soon will you marry me?"

"As soon as you want . . . how does yesterday sound?"

"As soon as possible sounds better, unless"—he held her away and looked at her seriously—"you want to wait until Sheryl and Robbie can come . . ."

She shook her head. "No. We've waited long enough, Logan, two long years. I don't want to wait any longer."

He moved to kiss her again, but she put her hands on his chest and held him away. "Logan, about the money . . ."

He laid her back on the bed and followed her down. "I'll be repaid when I see Robbie strong and well, out here riding a horse . . ."

And somehow, she knew Robbie would be strong and well. She could see him in her mind's eye now, perched in a saddle, laughing down at her and at the new little girl cousin Catriona held in her arms, a baby girl with Logan's eyes and her own dark hair . . .

"Catriona." There was a husky demand, a brand of passion in his voice that she would never be free of.

"Yes?"

"Take your case off the bed."

"Why?" she asked with mock innocence.

His hand moved sensuously up her thigh. "Why do you think?" he countered, his voice rough.

"Because you want a tidy wife?"

He looked down into her laughing face, his eyes caressing her. "No. I have a housekeeper to keep things tidy. I have a much more complicated requirement."

His fingers moved over the silk dress, finding the zipper at her nape. Curious, she asked, "What is this . . . mysterious requirement?"

"I need a wife who can sing our children to sleep." His smile was complacent.

She smiled up at him. "I might be able to manage that . . ."

He lowered his head to her. "Yes," he murmured huskily, "I thought you might."

LOOK FOR NEXT MONTH'S
CANDLELIGHT ECSTASY ROMANCES™

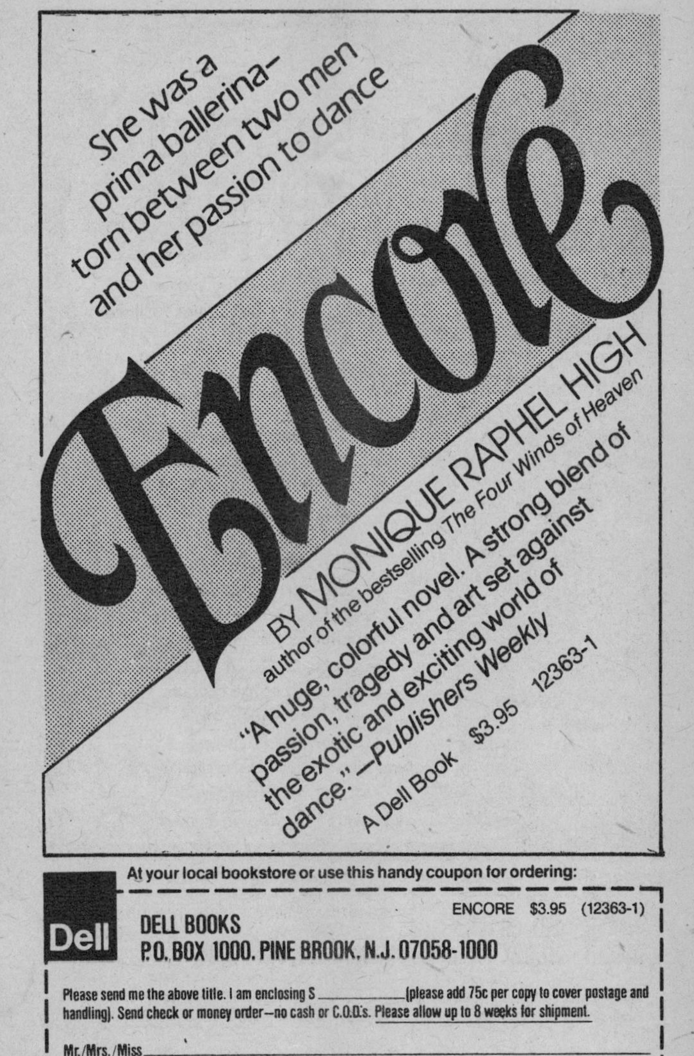
She was a
prima ballerina–
torn between two men
and her passion to dance
Encore
BY MONIQUE RAPHEL HIGH
author of the bestselling The Four Winds of Heaven
"A huge, colorful novel. A strong blend of
passion, tragedy and art set against
the exotic and exciting world of
dance." —Publishers Weekly
A Dell Book $3.95 12363-1